# In The House

# In The House

Lynn K. Kilpatrick

FC2

TUSCALOOSA

The University of Alabama Press
Tuscaloosa, Alabama 35487-0380

Published by FC2, an imprint of the University of Alabama Press, with
support provided by the Publications Unit of the Department of English
at Illinois State University, and the School of Arts and Sciences, University
of Houston–Victoria

Address all editorial inquiries to: Fiction Collective Two, University of
Houston–Victoria, School of Arts and Sciences, Victoria, TX 77901-
5731

⊗

The paper on which this book is printed meets the minimum requirements
of American National Standard for Information Sciences—Permanence
of Paper for Printed Library Materials, ANSI Z39.48–1984

Library of Congress Cataloging-in-Publication Data
Kilpatrick, Lynn K. (Lynn Kathleen)
In the house / Lynn K. Kilpatrick. — 1st ed.
    p. cm.
Short stories.
ISBN-13: 978-1-57366-154-6 (pbk. : alk. paper)
ISBN-13: 978-1-57366-815-6 (ebook)
1. Man-woman relationships—Fiction. I. Title.
PS3611.I452816 2010
813'.6—dc22
                                        2009038688

Book Design: Michael Bunce and Tara Reeser
Cover Design: Lou Robinson
Typeface: Garamond
Produced and printed in the United States of America

For Jason & Ross

"In The House" appeared in *Hotel Amerika*; "The Guy Who Planted Those Flowers" and "Temptations" appeared in *Spork*; and "On Understanding," "Bitter on the Tongue," and "How Things End" appeared in *Denver Quarterly*.

I would like to thank everyone at FC2 and University of Alabama Press, especially Lance Olsen, Ralph Berry, Brenda Mills, and Carmen Edington. This book would not exist without the support and guidance of Karen Brennan. I would also like to thank the University of Utah English Department, especially Katie Coles, Howard Horwitz, Steve Tatum, and Melanie Rae Thon. I am especially grateful for my family, my first readers and fans: Dell Taylor, John Kilpatrick, Kristi, Lisa, Erin, and their families. Thanks to Sylvia Torti and Nicole Walker for reading numerous versions of this collection. Thanks to friends whose encouragement and feedback keep me going: Rae Meadows, Steve Tuttle, Felicia Olivera, Brian Kubarycz, Lisa Bickmore, Dave McGlynn, Margot Singer, Rachel Marston. Thanks to the Utah Arts Council.

# Table Of Contents

In The House                                    13

My Neighbors                                    21

The Guy Who Planted Those Flowers               35

Dioramas Of The Domestic Landscape             37
    Window #1

Women In Confined Spaces                        39

Dioramas Of The Domestic Landscape             47
    Window #2

On Understanding                                49

Dioramas Of The Domestic Landscape             63
    Window #3

How Things End                                  65

The Infinite Cages                              69

Dioramas Of The Domestic Landscape             79
    Window #4

Bitter On The Tongue                            81

Dioramas Of The Domestic Landscape             87
    Window #5

After: Crime Scene 89

Knives In The Kitchen 91

The Third Suspect 97

Miss America: A Story In Sestinas 99

Dioramas Of The Domestic Landscape 113
    Window #6

Temptations 115

Dioramas Of The Domestic Landscape 119
    Window #7

Domestic Drama 121

*The covers of the book are like a roof and four walls. What is to happen next will take place within the four walls of the story.*

—John Berger

# In The House

**front porch:** *second person*

The story begins here.

As she stands poised, about to enter, our heroine is on the verge of transformation. Once she opens the door, events will be put in motion, actions will begin to occur. Once she opens the door, she will begin the inevitable change that will lead to her conclusion. Once she enters the house, she becomes a different person.

We know something about our heroine already: how she seems like you, the reader; how you'll slowly begin to see the world through her eyes. Even when she's *she*, she's *me*.

You know what's about to happen because you've been here before. But she hasn't. She's only just beginning: carefully walking up the front steps, placing her hand on the doorknob, pausing a moment to think.

We can observe her now. See? She's about to push the door open and begin. As the door creaks open, it's already too late.

**split-level entry:** *choices*

Up is the kitchen, with its assortment of motives, the dining room, a long hallway, all the bedrooms and their unmade beds. Downstairs is dirty: the laundry, the garage, the unfinished basement with its carpet remnants and castoff couches. Down is the realm of children, cement floors scattered with half-loved toys, cardboard houses, incomplete puzzles.

Upstairs belongs to her.

**foyer:** *pause*

Sooner or later, she'll have to choose. She bites her lip and appears to consider. Surrounded by doors and stairs and windows, she bides her time and breathes.

**stairs:** *rising action*

She hates the gold shag carpet.

**kitchen:** *conflict*

There's a secret he's keeping. On the counter, a butcher block with a chef's knife, a bread knife, sharpener. In the refrigerator, three kinds of beer and half a dozen mustards. In the spice cabinet: cinnamon, cloves, cayenne. He knows how to make a coffee cake from scratch and what to use to inspire sneezing, coughing, burning eyes, an ailment that looks like the flu, how to induce a miscarriage, how to seduce and tease.

She's making dinner. She possesses secrets of her own, different from his. She lets him stand behind her as she uses a knife on the meat, cutting through the muscle, avoiding bone. She doesn't worry about the names, only: sharp, sharper. Only the way her finger bleeds when she slices through skin, and the blood spreads and she can't tell her own blood from the ooze of the meat. She doesn't yell or call out. It's only an accident, as so many things are.

**hallway:** *a preposition*
> against a textured wall
> away from the kitchen
> around the corner
> behind a door
> beside the light switch
> close to
> down the empty hallway
> into the darkened corridor
> next to the bathroom
> out of the bedroom
> away from

**master bedroom:** *plot*

He's holding her down against the bed. What is she saying? Listen closely. You need to know what she wants, what she calls out as he presses his mouth over hers. Something is happening. Everyone is waiting, watching: him, her, you. Observing the ways in which they manipulate each other's bodies and then wait for a response, another event to follow the first.

Think of what happened in the kitchen. He has secrets, things he's not telling, the ways he moves her into the bedroom in the first place, with recipes and lies. The way she's supposed to want it and not want it. The secrets she has, what's beneath her pillow, what's under her shirt, between the sheets, inside her top drawer between her socks.

This is what brings events to where they are: he's holding her down and she's struggling, but struggling is so often interpreted as surrender.

**closet:** *dramatic questions*

Who is he?

What *happens* and what is simply *imagined?*

Did the woman scream or moan?

How will she get out of the bedroom?

What is she doing in the closet?

Will the children think to look in the closet?

What children?

**children's room:** *subplot*

The beds are much smaller, but aside from that it's like any other bedroom, any other room, with its books on the floor: *Your A to Z Guide to The Opposite Sex*, or *Where the Wild Things Are.*

There are seemingly abandoned stuffed animals still clutched in darkness. The worn spot in the carpet where the dog sleeps every night and where he turns his ritual circles before lying down and fixing his eyes on the young girl asleep beside him. He barks in his sleep and when she awakens he is always watching so that she begins to wonder if he sleeps at all, but that's his job, to watch and guard and to ensure that no one disappears, that there are no unexplained events, that each and every event has a beginning and a clear, discernible resolution.

**bathroom:** *first person*

This is the site of concealment, where the door locks and the layers are shed: clothing, makeup, jewelry, barrettes. She becomes an *I* again, or *I* become her, who knows really? But there she is, in the mirror, stripped down to the barest secret of skin taut over bones, where nothing can be concealed from the mirror and the harsh lighting, the cruel gaze of the cotton swab and tweezers.

The scale is pushed back beneath the counter, under the sink, no need for weighing and measuring when everything is so revealed. I have only to look in order to see the purple rising on her arms, the places where skin has been rubbed raw, the nicks and cuts, the abrasions, the curves where she should have stopped, and the hollows where she should have kept going.

How there is always too much and not enough and how in this light the reasons are so obvious, but when I flip the switch, there she is, I can't see anything and this nothing fills the whole room.

**front room:** *clues*

There are large brass candlesticks on the mantle. Some scraps of paper and ash in the fireplace. What is beneath the couch, ordered from a catalog and delivered to just this spot? Beside the couch, matching chairs and a large throw rug. Photographs of the children in various stages of development, black and white wedding photographs in which everyone smiles and looks as if they are trying to smile.

The room echoes with conversation and arguments. She might be sitting in the armchair reading a magazine but she's saying to him, *no* and *that's exactly what I thought you were going to say.*

If he has secrets, she has habits, the way her leg dangles over her knee and the rhythm with which she slowly moves her foot. The perfectly timed flipping of pages and the way she seems to hum without thinking about it. How long she waits before standing up and moving around, rearranging the cups on the coffee table, shuffling the newspapers, calling to the dog, *here boy, here.* The slight tilting of her head as she listens for sounds from far off, as if thunder might be moving in, as if anticipating the picture window's inevitable shatter into a hundred glittering eyes.

**attic:** *climax*

A woman screams. This sound is always attributed to the attic, that way no one has to go up and investigate. It could be the ghost of a dead woman or it could be a crazy woman or a woman who is alive and screaming for a reason. Because of violence or pain or emotional suffering. She has many reasons to scream.

She pretends not to hear. She hears the screaming and believes the sound may originate inside her own body. She is so often confused that she cannot remember if she heard the screaming or if she is a product of it.

He says he doesn't hear a thing, *come back to bed.*


**stairs:** *pace*

One false step might send her hurtling downward faster than she expected.


**basement:** *flashback*

The photographs of young girls in lilac dresses (this is someone else's childhood); odd socks (mismatched, abandoned); remnants of toys (doll arm, bear missing eyes, earless rabbit); desire (it was once so free, she often happened upon it, a catch in her throat, now it retreats from her as she searches, where can it be?); matched ivory washer and dryer (automatic, self-timing, silent); an old playhouse (solitary, one is an only child in the basement); her own distant childhood (the whole thing took place outdoors and entirely in summer, it was never dark, never snowed).


**sliding glass doors:** *allegory*

See the house to the north? That's where the happy couple lives. They have two dogs and no kids. They are always tan and always running laps around the neighborhood, waving and displaying their general good health. They are always throwing tennis balls and saying *good dog, good dog.* They drive white cars, and paint their house white, and their dogs are white, their jogging outfits white.

In two years the husband will come home one night and find his wife at the kitchen table eating lasagna. He will pull a chef's knife out of the butcher block and force it through her white shirt and into her body, blood spilling all over the table and the white carpet. Then he will drive away and on Monday they will find her body. After a six-state manhunt, they will give up looking for him. He will be happily remarried and living in Arkansas in a split-level rambler.

Either that or they will get a divorce and sell the house. The people who move in will not be nearly so happy. They will not wave or throw balls for their dogs. Instead they will have barbecues in their backyard that will erupt with laughter and then later shouting. The police will come and things will get quiet and then a few hours later the shouting will resume and then it will stop.

It is the way things go, the waving and the shouting. The houses are soundproof now, so whatever goes on inside stays in there, sealed up inside the rooms and spaces no one visits. That is one of the other stories.

**back door:** *conclusion*

Here she is again, her hand poised on the doorknob, about to move, to set events in motion. Or cause them to cease. That is so much more difficult. How do events stop arriving, one after the other, like a series of lightning strikes? She can't simply stand behind the door and ignore them. The events will find her.

How will she get out of the house? Perhaps she could kill herself, using the contents of a bottle simply labeled *solutions*. Or maybe someone could come to the door. Nothing so simple as the postman, or a person delivering a package. A woman. A neighbor, perhaps, who simply comes over as a diversion, in order to borrow something. Something to read.

# My Neighbors

### 1. Stella

I see her visiting the ATM next to Pei Wei and ten minutes later she is in the liquor store. She purchases a Cab and two Merlots. All her items are bagged in brown paper. She does not make eye contact as she passes.

### 2. Maggie

She is looking for shoes. She pauses at each window and looks in, running her finger across her lower lip. She is looking for something black, not too high, classy, fashionable, but something she can walk in for more than two blocks. Is that so impossible?

### 3. John

Bacon. Sausage. Turkey. Hamburger.
A few Granny Smiths.

## 4. Sam

I am worried about him. He hasn't bought anything for days. I peer through the blinds thinking he is on his way to Albertsons. But he is only walking his dog.

## 5. Penelope

She frequents the expensive knitting and sewing store in the upscale shopping center several blocks from our street. I am sometimes afraid of the sharp objects I spy jutting out of her bags. She often purchases needles, yarn, and fabric that she transports in several trips from her car to her house. Though she goes often to the store, I never see her wearing a sweater or anything that looks even remotely handmade.

## 6. Questions

Why do they have such normal names? Penelope is not all that common, I suppose. But don't people have more exotic names these days? Sam? In spite of their normalcy, I try to make them complex. I watch them closely, look for signs that they exceed the confines of their names. I carefully describe them, so as to indicate their fears and motivations.

## 7. John

When he leaves the house (he was obviously on his way to the store), I follow him there, and up and down the aisles. He seems not to notice me. He spends several minutes mulling over various cuts of meat: rib eye, London broil, pot roast. I imagine the dishes he will concoct: a Sunday roast with carrots and potatoes; stew with onions and peas. He chooses several packages wrapped in plastic and tosses them in his cart with a satisfying plop. His other items rattle and roll about. He selects one bag of salad and a bottle of creamy dressing, croutons, a six-pack of beer. When I think he's looking at me, I pretend to be reading the label of a soup can. "Hullo?" he says. I turn and quickly walk away.

## 8. Stella

She comes and goes with paper bags. I never see her put anything in the recycling bin. I make a note to mention it to her, though I never see her in daylight hours and even if I did, I would not speak to her. I see her at the liquor store. That's about it. Once I thought I saw her at a coffee shop, but it turned out not to be her, but rather her doppelgänger. I make a note to mention to her that she has a doppelgänger, who was wearing some very fashionable black boots. Maybe she should get some like that. But we both know that wine and black boots don't mix.

## 9. Methods

I sit on a hard wooden chair in front of the large window. The blinds are closed. In the morning, I quietly wait for noises in the street. Then I do one of several things: I listen and make notes. I peer through the blinds and observe, turning occasionally to my notebook for short periods of writing. I sit in the dark.

## 10. Sam

Sam only leaves his house to walk his dog. Sam is wasting away in a manner that is quite fashionable these days and involves jeans with skinny legs, white t-shirts, black hats, and skin so pasty you could write a suicide note on it. Oh Sam. I take a grocery store flier out of the recycling bin, circle a few healthy items like Bran Flakes and cottage cheese. I slip it under his door.

## 11. John

When the weather is fine, John barbecues. John barbecues meat products and nothing but meat products. I observe from across the street. If he looks up, I write something in my notebook. So far I have written *the smell of flesh burning* and *what if he never looks away?* When I look up, he is mowing the grass next to his grill. The smoke from his grill wafts into the house next door and a woman, she must be Laura, comes out and tells him to knock it off! He smiles and rubs a hand across his crazy hair. He offers her a hot dog and she accepts. They sit on the front steps eating hot dogs together and laughing. I write down *laughter.* When it gets dark, they walk to the store. I do not follow them. I know they are going to buy condoms. And maybe beer.

## 12. Maggie

The next time I see Maggie, she is wearing pink high heels and a black skirt. She leans into her car to extract her packages. She carries five or six bags into her apartment, leaving the door open. I can almost see inside. The one thing I can see is the bar in her kitchen, which is covered with magazines, videos, and beer cans. I want to know what goes on in there, to be able to say for sure how the beer cans became empty, what methods she uses for stacking her accumulated wealth. Tell me, I want to say with my eyes. But instead I close my blinds and sit in the dark.

## 13. Stella

I sometimes think Stella is my friend the way we glimpse each other on the sidewalk and do a dance of two steps over and one step back. She sometimes drinks wine right out in the driveway as if no one can see what she is doing. But I see her. I think she knows that. Once, when I saw her in the liquor store, I was holding a bottle of wine and my mouth was hanging open. She just smiled and said, "Oh, that's a good one." I said nothing. I bought the bottle of wine because I forgot what I was doing, and then I came home and drank the whole thing and slept until noon. The next day I saw Stella in the driveway with a wine glass in one hand doing the salsa to some music she must have imagined, except the way she swayed her hips I could hear it too and I almost started dancing and singing but right at the last minute I remembered I was me instead of Stella.

## 14. Tools

Notebook. Blinds. Pencil. Chair. Ears. Ability to know what others are thinking by the way they close their doors, swing their hands as if they are accessories, open their eyes in the morning. Eyes.

## 15. Sam

I might be in love with Sam, except he has a dog and dogs eat way too much. I see Sam lugging a bag of dog food home over his shoulder like it was a dead person. But it's not a dead person. He says, "Here Fletcher, here doggie." I think I might go buy a dog, but then I would have to walk it and then I could not sit here and watch Sam walk his dog, and his dog might smell my dog and then Sam would say what's her name? And I would have to answer. I might ask him, what kind of food do you give him? I hear him calling the dog, day and night, "Fletcher, Fletcher." Why did he name the dog Fletcher? I do not know. To find the answer, I would have to speak to Sam. I want to ask him, Why did you name your dog Fletcher? But such questions could lead to other things, like conversations and kisses in the dark.

## 16. Stella

Stella might have a boyfriend who is a vampire, because I only see him at night, going in and out of doors like an idea. His clothing is all black and I watch him kiss her with all the curtains open. He likes her in certain ways, I know, but he never brings her food or takes her to the store. Sometimes he walks across the street for ice cream, but she stays inside. She is shy like me, except when she drinks wine in the street. She dances inside too, and I can hear her singing. She calls my name and waves, but she is only washing her windows in the bright, bright sun.

## 17. Penelope

I want to believe Penelope is a kind and giving person, but she might be a dangerous individual. She does not leave her house much, and when she does, she carries large non-descript items wrapped in white paper into her house. I never see her eat, and if she does so, she must close her curtains. She leaves the newspaper on the front steps until noon and she must wait until the one minute I am not watching to leave the house, because somehow she always sneaks out and comes back later. She may be crazy or in-dependently wealthy. She likes to rake leaves early in the morning, the rake scratching against the sidewalk like a cat in heat.

## 18. John

I like John less the longer I watch him. Is it realistic for him to eat so much meat? He likes to walk over to the store and tote his bags back like a hunter. He leaves bloody garbage for the dogs to fight over, and then they spread the evidence up and down the street. I have seen the red paper towels. I know. He goes in and out at all hours and he can't always be hungry. Can he? How many calories a day does the average man need?

## 19. Maggie

Maggie drives up and down the street as if she were shopping for soup. She stops in front of each house and looks up into the eaves. Then she drives to the next one. In front of mine, she stops and gets out of her car. When I hear her knock, my heart takes a break. I lie on the floor and do deep breathing. She does not call out, but only leaves something on a mat I have that says *don't treat me like a doormat*. She leaves her business card. She's a real estate agent. Buy a house from ME! her card exclaims. It turns out her name is not Maggie.

## 20. Stella

Stella has not brought any bags home for three full days. I suspect that she will be moving out soon. I might call the landlord if it did not mean that I would have to speak to him. But why should I care? She has stopped dancing and drinking wine in the driveway. I saw her last week at the liquor store. She had a grocery cart full of red wine and also an extra large bottle of tequila. I wanted to say Arriba! as I passed her with my bottle of white. But I could not. I could not bring myself to say it.

21. Abstract

My neighbors are nothing special. They are ordinary. They come and go like geese.

22. Penelope

Tell me something, Penelope. What does a single woman want with such packages? I suspect they may be from the butcher, but we do not have a butcher in our neighborhood. Where is she driving for such things? I check the yellow pages, but they give no answers. Penelope has craft projects and lumpy white packages. Next year, I suppose, she will hang up a sign offering quilt blocking or some such thing. I want to see her tuck her auburn hair behind her ear. Just to see if it is something she would do.

23. Sam

Sam no longer walks the dog or whistles his tunes. He is paler than usual and he needs some iron. Eventually he has to go to the store, of course, and I am ready. I wear a dark coat and a blue hat with sunglasses. He gets a cart which he puts dog food in and also beer. I get some frozen spinach and when I almost accidentally bump his cart, I drop it in. Maybe he will not buy it, but my guess is he will be too distracted at the checkout line by the sight of a policeman stopping a young woman in a dark coat and glasses as she tries to leave the store without paying for her purchases. What stuff? she'll be saying. What stuff?

24. Stella

Halloween is my only chance. I am short. I have a black skirt and some white tights. I walk behind young children and stand on the bottom step as if I am the older sister. I look down and shake my head when they offer candy, but I can see right inside. Stella, can't you see me seeing you? Her front door opens up into a room filled with newspaper and empty bottles. Oh Stella. She pushes the door almost closed. "What do you want?" she says to me. Just then a child runs up and yells, "Trick or treat!" I smile and back away.

## 25. Maggie

Maggie puts a sign up in a yard down the street. It says *Open House.* I wait all week for Saturday and then I wait until two cars drive up at the same time. I walk in behind them and Maggie barely notices. I don't take one of the cookies that are on the dining room table. I stand in every room when it is empty and twirl around as if it were my own. Maggie peeks her head in and says, "Any questions?" I turn around and around. The two couples eye each other suspiciously as they pass in the hallway. "How much?" says one. "How much are they asking?" Maggie turns and smiles. She likes to talk dollar amounts.

## 26. Sam

Sam does not come out of his house. He has his food delivered in various vehicles. I fear he is dying or dead. I miss watching his travels up and down the street, imagining what his hand might feel like, cool and limp, in mine. His dog runs around in the yard and sometimes goes into the street. "Here doggie," I whisper. But he cannot hear me because we are separated by glass and so many yards of street and grass.

27. Penelope

Oblivious to my predictions, Penelope does nothing. The days go on and on. She goes to the store only on Tuesdays, when the store offers a senior discount. She buys bags of apples. She pushes her groceries home in a cart. Hey lady, I think, that's illegal.

28. Distance

I mustn't talk to them or interfere in any way. If I interact with them, I may influence their behavior. They may do something differently, because they do or do not sense me here, waiting for what they will do next. Is this how the great apes felt, being watched as they ate, slept, fornicated? My neighbors seem a bit like gorillas. I can discern no great longings or intellectual discomfort. What if they are simply content and go on like this, never altering their course?

29. John

What does he do in the winter? The smell of cooked meat must overpower him. He lies on the couch, sleeping with his clothes on. Or he reads, though I have never seen him buying a book, or coming home from the library. Does he dream? Does he ache from hunger? What does he see with his eyes closed?

30. Stella

She no longer dances in the driveway. There is snow on the ground. She retreats inside. Does she dance there? I must assume she does not, for I cannot see her, and try as I might I cannot hear the sounds of music or the click her heels might make on kitchen tiles. She no longer brings items out for the recycling, and she does not leave the door open so that I might briefly glimpse the inside. I can only conclude that she no longer dances, no longer sings, but stays alone, drinking.

## 31. Maggie

She moves outside in the sunlight. Unlike the others, she sticks to a routine. She leaves the house in her professional apparel at 8:30 each morning. She waves to people on the street and she yields to oncoming traffic. I watch until she turns at the corner, merging with the other vehicles. Her head bobs as she listens to music. She does something else. She smiles.

## 32. Sam

In spite of my better instincts, I think about Sam. I miss his voice calling out to the dog. I miss the dog. An observer is not supposed to become involved with her subjects whether they are ants, equations, or people. But Sam has retreated so far into himself that he has disappeared. His apartment remains dark. Perhaps he is a black hole, and all available light bends toward him. Where has he gone? Nowhere. He is still somewhere, even if only in my mind.

## 33. Penelope

She could knit an afghan large enough to cover us all, those of us who are cold and alone. Instead, she stays inside. I imagine she labors, day and night, trying to find a way to warm everyone. She has work, just as I do. But in the daylight, what do either of us have to show for it?

## 34. John

I almost wish for spring, so that John could be outside again, grilling, drinking beer, and waving to the neighbors. Maybe he could get Sam to come outside, offering food to him and the dog. Stella would be there too, and Maggie. Only Penelope and I would stay away, at a safe distance. I'd like for it to happen, though I recognize that it never will.

## 35. Sam

I imagine walking into Sam's apartment. He has left the door unlocked. He expects me. I fix him soup and feed it to him in bed. Fletcher sleeps in the living room, his sides heaving in sleep. We do not speak, Sam and I, but we understand each other, as if in a dream or a parallel world. I touch his white skin and he does not make a sound, but looks deep into me with black eyes. I alter the course of events with my desire.

## 36. Stella

Stella is alone. She moves about in the dark of her apartment. She drinks wine from a large goblet, being careful not to spill. Newspapers cover the floor and she makes noise when she walks, like a mouse moving through fall leaves. The dark comforts her, as does the dark taste of wine. She never sleeps, but keeps moving, pacing circles through her life. This is where she is now.

## 37. Penelope

I could almost be Penelope, except I stay inside, safe behind the window with my notebook. We hide, as if we can stop events by ignoring them. Penelope goes to the store and returns. Every day she reads the paper. She has been known to smile or wave at a neighbor. She does not act as I predict, nor does she follow my instructions. She does what she chooses and mostly outside of my view.

## 38. Maggie

Maggie continues to exceed my descriptions. She moves about happily, and with no regard for intention or consequence. First she calls herself something other than Maggie, then she smiles, as if she is in control. I cannot describe what she will do next, nor determine why. She will not behave.

## 39. John

I have erased John from this neighborhood by simply ceasing to record his behavior and activities. His world no longer intersects with mine or with that of the others. I have eliminated him.

## 40. Sam

Though he no longer appears outdoors, I continue to narrate his behavior as if nothing has changed. Today he smiled as he walked Fletcher past my window. He moved his hand in an arc as if to wave. His feelings for me are developing.

## 41. The End

I know my neighbors, in the way that only an observer can understand the signs concealed in everyday gestures. They buy items, consume food, sing. I bestow meaning on their lives by determining, day after day, what they are doing. I am always watching, whether or not they turn their heads to notice me. I observe and record their behavior. My notebook is ready.

# The Guy Who Planted Those Flowers,

those pink geraniums, in the flower box outside my front door, may or may not be a bartender. He may or may not stop by three times a week to water them. I never see him.

The guy who planted those flowers is a DJ at the community radio station. He is the star of his own Irish film. His show is called *The Celtic Dragon* and every Sunday at three he plays the same songs; these songs form the soundtrack of the film that may or may not be his life.

He likes me because I'm Irish. I told him my last name and he blushed. I leaned in and said "I'm a poet." I may or may not have been lying. He likes me because I'm a writer of Irish ancestry and he may or may not be, right at this moment, thinking of me, dialing my number or writing me a poem.

I should never have let him in. A few weeks ago, some friends and I were leaving a bar with a case of Lucky's and he tagged along. He was invited by my friend who happens to be in a band with him. We went to my apartment and drank the whole case of beer and ate leftover chili on saltine crackers.

This may or may not have been when he saw the dead flowers in the flower box outside my door. This was when he discovered I was a poet. I may or may not have been drunk.

The guy who planted those flowers, he and I live in a small town. Example: a friend of mine with curly red hair and a British boyfriend enchanted this same man. Her voice has a slight lilt from her ongoing conversations with said British boyfriend and this lilt may or may not pass for an Irish accent. This accent definitely contributed to the obsession that the guy who planted those flowers had with her.

The guy who planted those flowers cannot remember my best friend's name though they have both lived in this town for six years. She says it may or may not have to do with the fact that she is in possession of certain facts about his past escapades. Apparently his ex-girlfriend was Irish, had curly red hair, and left him for another man that she may or may not have met while traveling in Europe. I remember, at least, that their breakup had something to do with postcards.

The guy who planted those flowers is stalking me.

# Dioramas Of The Domestic Landscape

## Window #1

A miniature couple, small, smaller than you might think. I know you are imagining humans the size of Barbie, but really, that's not small enough. Think of Army men, in their small fatigues, with binoculars and guns. That small. Only they're a couple, a man and a woman. They stand in a terrain shaped from modeling clay and construction paper. The hills in the background are painted red, and the sky is a baby blue that only paper can be. The man holds out his hand to the woman as if saying something. As if his outstretched arm is sign enough. The woman stands, hands at her sides. She observes the man, the modeling clay landscape, the sky that opens like a shoebox. She seems to want for nothing. Though she is plastic, and entirely red, she seems content. Almost happy.

# Women In Confined Spaces

*Elevators*

She avoids elevators because they tend to be small, with décor that reminds her of a casket or the parlors of funeral homes.

*The Academy*

In graduate school, she gravitated toward the other women with short hair. She presumed that the students with short hair would have a stronger sense of self and be able to navigate the difficult corridors of higher education with less damage to their self-images. She sees now that this assumption was misguided, that short hair was just one among many uniforms to choose from and that it was chosen with as much caprice as any other disguise, such as long hair, bangs, expensive handbags, or cosmetic surgery.

*Department Stores*

She appreciates department stores for their clear divisions, the various fashions separated off from each other in mini-boutiques with names like "Tweens" or "Women's." She can't decide which she is, so she wanders aimlessly, rubbing different fabrics between her fingers as if she understands any but the most obvious distinctions, like those between velvet and wool. She is occasionally bothered by the lack of windows, though this same timelessness is part of the store's appeal. When she emerges, blinded, it could be noon or it could be midnight. How would she know? In the department store, she feels as if it is always morning, a perpetually groggy environment that necessitates large doses of caffeine and marzipan. There is a small café in the department store, so she doesn't even have to leave, she can stay all day, consuming three meals here, ricocheting from housewares, with its shiny black espresso machines, to bedding, which has actual beds, where she could sleep if she wanted to, if that salesman in the stiff, blue suit would leave her alone and stop asking her, "What are you looking for ma'am, something for you and your husband, do you have kids?" But she ends up in "Professional Closet," seriously mulling over a skirted suit with a jacket designed to make her boobs look bigger. And then lingerie, where all the bras are padded, and she wonders if that huge chunk of money she spent on graduate school would not have been better spent on a boob job (size C), a black bikini, and a week in Oaxaca.

*Closets*

As a child, she used to hide in her mother's closet. She loved the scent of White Shoulders that clung to the silky dresses and soft sweaters. She thought if her mother had secrets they would be hidden there, but she never found anything surprising, nothing even remotely jarring, which now, in her own advancing years, disturbs her even more than some old forgotten love letters or naked pictures could. Her mother had no secrets. She makes a mental note to hide something in her own closet, just in case she dies suddenly and her own mother must come over to clean out her house. She wants her mother to know that she is nothing like her.

*Families*

Are families small, claustrophobic spaces or wide open ones, causing the agoraphobic to claw at her own throat, retreat to a small room with only a desk, a chair, and a bed? Her own family, she decides, is both. Simultaneously stifling and distant, in a way that makes her think of a one-room cabin on an endless plain. She could never reach her arms around all of them, spread as they are across the continental United States, and yet, when the phone rings, she has to consider for a moment what she is willing to endure. Sometimes, when she hears a voice on the other end, with its inquiries and emotional demands, she feels the weight of a heavy quilt on her chest, as if she were crouched down in her childhood bed with every blanket on top of her. Wasn't that supposed to feel good? The blankets, the coziness? Instead it is a kind of enveloping liberation, a freedom that constricts. Like when she lets the dog out in the yard, and instead of running around in the open middle space, he runs laps around the perimeter. She always imagines he's thinking, what about here? what about here?

So this represents the culmination of her long years in the library, slavishly pouring her heart into obscure theoretical convolutions which only a small handful of other scholars can understand. She owns a charming Craftsman cottage, approximately 1,200 square feet, three and a half blocks from the local coffee shop and 100 yards from a chain grocery store where she can buy beer, but not wine. What's the point of all this thinking if at the end of the day she can't buy frozen dinners and a nice Chardonnay without having to get in her car and drive to the state liquor store? And what about the endless debates over intelligent design and evolution, or whether gay high school students can have their own clubs or not? Did she spend countless hours parsing the meaning of the word *woman* so that conservative ne'er-do-wells could assert that each word has only one meaning, agreed upon by them? What is the point anymore? She doesn't even have any wine in the house with which to console herself.

*Commuter Train*

What happened to common courtesy? Was it really necessary, for example, to be forced to overhear the conversation of a man on his cell phone telling someone, "Don't cry, honey. No, stop. Stop crying"? At first she thinks he must be talking to a child, with his condescending tone, and there, there attitude. Then she realizes it is his wife when he says, "Listen. Go to the neighbors. I'll pick you up there. They can take care of you. Should I pick up some wine?" What happened to private conversations? She realizes there is no such thing now, that every conversation is public, and as such, subject to public scrutiny.

Does this give her the right, then, to turn to him and say, "I give that marriage six months. If a man ever talked to me that way, I'd deck him"? But she realizes, too, that the woman might want to be spoken to that way, with the little coos and *honey*s as if she were still a child. This man and his cell phone have changed the small space of the train car into a roving phone booth, one that holds a hundred people, each having their own public, private conversation. She does not care, for example, what the man in the brown suit seated next to her is having for dinner. But she is forced to listen to, "Potatoes, right, got it. How about some green beans? Yep. And steak? Okay." Such conversations make her yearn for her tiny home, one room really, with a kitchen alcove and a closet bathroom, with hundreds of graduate school books that remain silent until opened. At least there she is not forced to witness these transgressions against the privacy clause, the foundation of modern civilization. There are two spaces, she thinks, inside and outside. Can't everybody see that?

*Marriage*

Marriage is something she observes from outside, like a latecomer staring in the large plate glass window at the party flourishing in her absence. Should she go in? Or is she content to see the others, leaning their heads back for long laughs that do not escape the enclosed space of the hostess's house? Through the window, she can see all the couples, identifiable by their resemblance to one another: the Blonde couple, the Tan couple, the Outdoorsy couple, the Quiet couple, and so on. Is it worth it, though, to break through the divide, to open the door and interrupt their camaraderie? Perhaps not. The gift wine in her hand becomes suddenly heavy. The house is just one more disguise, she decides. One more straitjacket masquerading as a down comforter. Or is it the other way around? She really shouldn't walk around her neighborhood at night, where conundrums might spring out at her from any domestic lawn. But when she does, just for a moment she feels free, anonymous, alone.

*Her Office*

The building is old, of course, and she has to climb three flights of stairs to get there, and then when she lands, huffing, in the ancient chair, there isn't even a window. But she should be glad just to have an office. Some of the other teachers meet with students in empty classrooms or hallways, having those uncomfortable encounters out in the open for everyone to see. She sits in her office, typing mostly, sometimes actually writing, and looks up whenever someone walks past. It is never any of her students, whom she fears she intimidates so much that they don't dare come by her office. Her office is overstuffed with theoretical books, and the texts she uses for her classes. Her office reflects neither her aesthetic nor her personal self, but a hybrid of what she's read and who she thinks she should be. On her door she has taped two postcards, one from her recent trip to Barcelona, of La Sagrada Familia, and another, from a friend, of an extremely busty woman from a farcical movie based on a comic book. What does it mean, she sometimes thinks, the juxtaposition of the two images? Perhaps this is why she sits alone during her office hours, reading and then deleting her email. No one can figure out the coded syntax of her office door. They do not know whether to approach her with humor or apprehension.

*The English Language*

When she was an undergraduate, she spelled woman with a y, but she always admired her peers who spelled it wimmin as if the chaos that brought them forth in this world as female was an action, *wimming*, from which they had simply dropped the g. She also loved to hear students in her Gender Studies class demand, "What about herstory? huh?" as if they had just, in their anger, coined the term. Lately, though, she prefers to think of words the same way she thinks of baggy, worn-out sweats. She wouldn't ever leave the house in them, but when she returns home at the end of the day she can't wait to put them on and watch some trashy TV, something she would never admit to watching, like *Entertainment Tonight* or reruns of *Mork and Mindy*. Language is like those sweats. She pretends they matter, and that they are the subject of much inquiry. But she longs to don them and just let them sag on her, hanging there, the elastic exhausted. Comfortable. That's it. In her head, she never worries about using the correct word. The conversations in her mind are long and convoluted, but she almost never pauses midsentence in there to think, wait, do I mean *theoretical* or *hypothetical*? Or what does *rhetorical* **mean** anyway? She loves to talk when no one can hear her.

*Hybrid Vehicles Manufactured In Asia*

She feels like such a cliché in her car, especially when she drives around her neighborhood, honking and waving at people just like her in similar cars. She most often spies herself in the parking lot of a local health food store or at the secondhand clothing store. In those moments, she feels herself leaving her body, floating, able to see herself as she really is: just one of many people who hope beyond logic that their actions have consequences, and who believe as they drive around with their cloth bags in the trunk, wearing recycled clothing, sporting tattoos, that their form of capitalism is somehow different.

*Her Own Body*

At night, when she's trying to sleep, she closes her eyes and listens to her own breathing. She swears she can feel the food moving through her, her blood flowing, unwillingly, from one organ to another. Sometimes she thinks she could stop anytime she desired, just make her mind up and cease breathing, with no blood or poisons or weapons. She tries to remember the kind of breathing she had to learn, to let go and let the breath come in, as if breath had a will of its own and could enter without her consent. "Don't think of your body as a house," a man once said to her, "you are your body." She hates him now, with a passion that borders on envy. What did he know about her body? Men were always touching her skin and marveling at its softness, the almost invisible down that covers her arms. She remembers the way he moaned, a whispery hum, and her stomach begins to retreat toward her spine. Even her body knows the truth, and she does not feel as if she is her body so much as her body is her. She is just a sum of her parts, an equation that does not add up, a collection of cells and hormones and biochemical reactions that make her think things such as, *what is the logic of negative numbers* and *how do I get out of here, this body in which I am trapped?*

# Dioramas Of The Domestic Landscape

## Window #2

In this one the people are represented by stick figures, made by simply gluing parts of Popsicle sticks to other Popsicle sticks. The eyes are represented by Xs or Os, and each person has yarn for hair, yellow or brown or black. All the sticks are the same color though, a woodenish beige that looks like a version of human skin. These people wear clothing on only one side of their bodies, mere sheets of fabric cut to approximate the idea of dress or pants or shirt. Their mouths are red slashes of marker near the top of the sticks. They have no ears. In this scene, the people stand around a flat surface that may be a bed. This bed consists of a medium-sized matchbox covered by a piece of blue felt. Two cotton balls pretend to be pillows. The people, with their expressionless mouths and lack of hands or feet, seem to be waiting for something. An event is about to happen, or perhaps has just occurred. They do not react, but simply perch, footless, next to the bed. One man, his mouth a perfect O, seems about to speak.

# On Understanding

*what I know*

She walked into my apartment and disrupted the cohesion of our group. We were circled around the playing board, itself a circle, asking each other questions from a box, knowledge which we then squirreled away for future reference. The three of us: me, my roommate, my boyfriend. We looked up and she was standing at the door holding a guitar case. She set it down in the middle of the room. She introduced new words into our conversation: moving, practice, rest. I want to say I invited her to join us. I want to say she felt welcome, but was in a hurry, had to go pack, was leaving tomorrow. Some of this is true; she was leaving. We were a circle, the three of us and she had walked into my apartment, disrupting. Or I had buzzed her up. Yes, I must have, but then, suddenly, she was a surprise, her presence, her absolute presence there in my doorway. Then she disappeared.

*she disappears*

This is literal. I understand, and when I say "understand," this is not theoretical, as in something I can pretend to grasp, like god or the theory of relativity, for the duration of our conversation. By "understand" I mean this: she is somewhere in darkness, money dampened by sweat clinging to the palm of her hand. The only time she touches another person is when this bill changes hands, when her fingers, accidentally and suggestively, caress the fingers of the man who slides a smoke-colored vial into her palm. I understand this the way I understand gravity. We don't get to believe or disbelieve, to prove or disprove. Some things just are and this is one of those things. I understand because she told me. One beer, then six. One hit, then two. She gave me the guitar and took her two weeks paid vacation. I understand this too, because people contemplating suicide give things away, often everything. What I don't understand is the gun.

*the gun*

The gun represents missing information, what I don't know, like the card in Clue that is carefully inserted into the solution envelope and promptly lost. Her face I can picture. Even how she might have looked, sprawled in a not unsexual way in the tall grass beside Lake Washington. And her voice. She talks with me in the 5 a.m. dark, damp with departing rain, her voice still a constant rasp. I try to picture the gun into her hand. Mornings on my way to work, I pass pawn shops and gun stores, fondling each gun in my mind, placing it into her still live hands. Her hands are sweaty and she knows, but she is steady and, most importantly, still alive. She wants a gun the way she wants booze or crack or anything hot that burns through her veins and the gun is all that. And this is when I first see her as she is, not as she was, alive and beside me every day. But as she is, in the true core of herself that is pure energy which never goes away, as just one body in a world full of forces. And it occurs to me that she was stable, fixed, until the idea of suicide put her in motion. She was a body at rest until this force began to act upon her.

*inertia: bodies at rest tend to stay at rest unless acted upon by an external force*

Perhaps I am oversimplifying. Perhaps it was not simply the gun acting upon her. But I can't ignore the gun. I can't theorize the gun into a letter in an equation, where $x = inertia$ and $y = the\ external\ force$. Solve for y. I am intimate with her inertia, her routine: she got up at 4:30 a.m. to ride her bike up Queen Anne hill. After work, she rode her bike to the pool and swam laps. She would return to her monkish dwelling. A mattress on the floor and a boom box. One hundred CDs from classical to rap. She would heat up canned soup in her only pot and eat it out of a mug. Near the end she would take the beer, six or twelve, sit on her mattress and listen to rap. This is where her plans begin.

*her plans*

Drunk, imprisoned—
oh, maybe melodramatic, but it was a large, brick building with
bars on the windows to keep people out and people in—listening to Ravel or Public Enemy. Picture her inertia, its qualities.
The texture of night, the thinness of the mattress, the coarse
nature of the sheets, the pervasive smell of must and decay, the
solitary light bulb. Where is the gun in all this? She is the inert
body; the idea that she can take her own life pressing against
her skin. Her inertia begins to move in a given direction. There
is an end destination to this vector of movement and as she
hurtles toward it, she sees the inevitable conclusion. She recog-
nizes the distinction between *slow train* and *rapid transit*. Within
this concept resides a whole range of activities I cannot picture her performing. She doesn't believe in checks or credit
cards, so she withdraws the necessary amount of cash. This
bundle chafes against her stomach in a secret money belt. She
exchanges money for the assurance that she can choose.

*she can choose*

Later, after they enter her empty apartment and tell me, after I continue going to work as usual, after everyone begins to forget, I learn about the receipt. This is how her brother knows she has a gun. He goes to her apartment and sifts through her belongings. I say sift because her things are so much sand between his fingers. Like the medium in which ancient treasures are found. He is searching as if he will find something long buried. Instead what he finds is a receipt for the gun and a note which tells her landlord that her brother will come and take away the things which she has boxed up. The things, that is, she has not given away. She has given me her couch. She has given a book to one of our customers. She has given her CDs to our boss. She has deposited her guitar in the middle of my living room floor. She has left her keys in her apartment and pulled the door closed behind her.

*she closes the door*
*behind her*

An external force moves her. She has gone away on vacation and returned. I am only speculating, but I think this is when she retrieves the gun. She picks up her last paycheck. It is cashed in Tacoma. There is no image of her on the bank's surveillance tape. I think she has already disappeared. Maybe she used the ATM to minimize her contact with human beings. She wouldn't want to touch the teller's hand, to think: this is what we have in common. She wouldn't want to think: I could just as easily kill you. This is not the direction of the idea. The idea spirals inward. The idea pushes her body in the direction of its own action.

*the body moves in the direction of action of the force*

She moves inward. Toward destruction. I picture a sinkhole on a river, a whirlpool, a black hole. She is pulled further and further inside of herself until what someone else might recognize is gone. She disappears. This is literal. When I say disappears, I am not saying that her whereabouts were unknown. She was somewhere in Washington, maybe even in Seattle. By disappear, I mean that she was not visible. I could not see her. In my dreams, I pass by her on the street every day. She puts out her hand for money but I shrink away, because I know where that money goes. I do not see her.

*I do not see*

This is what I mean by "I do not understand." This is what I mean by "disappear." This is what I mean by "the gun." This is what I mean by "smoke-colored vial." This is what I mean by "Tacoma." This is what other people mean by "personal problems." This is what other people mean by "immovable object" and "unstoppable force." This is what her parents mean by "god." This is what other people mean by "disappear." This is what other people mean by "euphemism." This is what I mean by "mean." This is what I mean by "external force." This is what I mean by "body."

*body*

  I wrote "sprawled in a not unsexual way" but I did not see the body. I did not attend the funeral. I did not wear black and stop to shake her parents' hands. I did not feel the cold beneath their flesh, as motionless as hers. I did not "try to make my peace with it." I did not go to work. I did not cry. I reread the birthday card she gave me. She wrote, "someone to say 'I'm glad you're alive' and I am!" I walked the streets and it would not even rain. I saw her on her bike, legs in motion, the sinewy muscles and flesh of her. The long thin music of her hands. I felt her death in the rain that refused to fall.

•

*to fall*

At work we pretended she was on some kind of extended vacation. I heard myself saying, "we don't know when she'll be back." I knew about the gun, her apartment, Tacoma. I tried to believe she had escaped. I knew she had not. The world around me expanded to fill her absence, the way water encircles an object that displaces it. The fog became just another palpable emotion like coffee and silver and knives. This is months before we would know. Know for sure. That is, if we chose to believe in police reports and evidence. But I already knew. I knew in the way the wind always blew into my face. The way she had always walked against the light. A force can only push so far before we begin to push against it.

*for every action*

*there is an equal and opposite reaction*

If a force spirals inside you, works its way beneath your ribs and into your lungs, how do you push against it? If there is motion in your blood, pounding and pulsing, what is its opposite? If the effect of drugs is called "high," how do you push against it? What is the last thought of a person pressing the cold "O" of the gun against her temple? What evidence do I have of an action opposite to her thought? What is the force that presses her body to the ground? What is its opposite? If it is true that the soul rises up after death, is the body pressing down with equal force? I imagine her heavy with death. I imagine gravity holding twice as fast to what remains. Her body exerting a force it never could in life. Whatever the action of death, whatever its direction of motion, I imagine that her body, silent in the grass, is its equal and opposite. In a situation like this, how do I define "force"?

*define force*

There is
a stillness at 5 a.m. There is a darkness. The tensions on either
side of these arbitrary descriptions hold such qualities in bal-
ance. For example, just beneath the stillness is tension; just
beyond the darkness, day. At 5 a.m., the darkness recalls her
to me exactly as she was when we arrived at work. The noises
of the city were moving toward us from a distance. All of the
light was artificial. Occasional traffic moved silently past our
window. She put on a classical tape. We said nothing, or little.
One day she didn't show up. And one day I found out. She
disappeared.

# Dioramas Of The Domestic Landscape

## Window #3

The bicycle is an ingenious device constructed from paper clips bent to look like wheels, handlebars, pedals, and a small seat. The bicycle lacks a rider, however, and lies precariously on a piece of black construction paper painted with yellow and white stripes. Beyond the bicycle and across a broad expanse of green, a flat house waits. The door is a flap that conceals, but nothing lies inside. Behind the door, which hangs open as if it didn't have the will to hide anything, as if it couldn't bear to remain closed, lies nothing, just space, the whole ruse revealed, it's someone's hand, or a piece of blank cardboard, or the edge of a desk. There aren't even any people in this one, only the absence of people. The bicycle might have been laid there by a small boy made only of toothpicks, a boy who always wanted a bicycle except that he's made of wood and glue, and any motion at all might cause him to collapse, becoming, finally and originally, simply what he is.

# How Things End

Right after. Things are over and you move on.

Months later. First we broke up and then we went to Thailand and then we came home and then we broke up again. Months later.

In the hotels, there were these little soaps shaped like hearts and shells, and I thought about them as we made love on a twin-sized bed. There was no air conditioning and it seemed like things could go on indefinitely.

The doctor warned us of rabies. They don't kill dogs over there, he said. They let them wander around the streets. They believe in an enduring soul, and they don't want to make the mistake of eliminating a good one.

We pretended to still love each other and the truth is I did still love him, the way I loved all the men I could no longer talk to. I felt nostalgia for him, though he was sitting right beside me.

We watched *Magnum, P.I.* with subtitles while we drank Heineken. It was raining on Koh Samui and we had to.

We ate rice three meals a day and began to believe in it.

I forgot about bread, strawberry jam, and soft pillows of butter, which had to do with the broken part, the part we left in our bags when we stripped down to our swimsuits and plunged into the water even though it was raining.

He tried to translate the dishes on the menu: *kha* was coconut, *tom* was soup, *gai* meant chicken.

Through goggles, he looked more familiar.

Before we went to Thailand, I made out with a guy we both knew, twice his size and blonde.

He asked, it's because I'm short, isn't it?

At the Golden Buddha, I fell on the rain-slick stairs and he walked right by me. Monks in their saffron robes orbited the shining Buddha. Tourists asked me in languages I didn't understand if I was hurt.

Remember the way he looked up over his glasses?

His stories were always allegories for sex and subterfuge. One featured a refrigerator and one a wooden doll.

On B—— Street in Bangkok, he ate Tom Kha Gai as I looked on. I was looking for a batik dress and I was distracted.

Can we go now? I asked.

The end was coming, had come and passed right over the table, was gone and would return.

The bruise from falling would endure, turning yellow, then green, and finally a deep, troubling purple.

We held hands and made jokes about fried silkworm larva.

He counted the number of times we saw a sign that read See Monkey Work Coconut.

I drank beer from a can and wore a wrap over my swimsuit. I sat in the sun and tried to burn.

I learned words that became obsolete.

Four months later, I took him out for Thai food and then we went to see *My Fair Lady*.

Desire gnawed inside of me, a small, rabid dog.

I bought a mango from an old woman on the beach just to watch her peel it.

In Surat Thani, I fell in love with our waitress. She brought me eggs and rice, with tomatoes disguised as flowers.

I didn't try the fish salt.

He reached out and grabbed my wrist. It didn't hurt. Not now, I said.

*Kha* meant many things: man, wood, okay.

He had left me a note, folded like origami, which read: I'm a coyote chewing off my paw.

I thought it meant he loved me.

I had to lift my feet up to avoid the water sweeping through the café. Don't worry, said the owner. I'll make you something delicious.

He wrote: There is something inside her which says she has to go.

After the movie, he forced his way inside my apartment and tried to kiss me. I said, there's someone else.

In Ao Nan, I bought a bottle of water every night and the woman laughed.

The red curry burned my tongue, made my eyes water.

I drank iced coffee only once because they were out of milk.

He said, don't write, don't try to contact me.

He called me every day.

After awhile, I forgot his last name.

# The Infinite Cages

The world was too big, Elaine thought. Her head was full of lilacs and the nearly inaudible scraping the beetles made as they moved across the basement floor. With her front door wide open, nearly anyone could enter. She considered this. From the basement, she would be able to hear his footsteps as he stomped across the floor. This someone could be almost anyone, even a husband.

Under the kitchen table felt bigger than it actually was. Mia had loved it as a child: brought all her stuffed bears, and the blanket that was white on one side and pink on the other and hid under there for hours. Elaine hardly knew where she was, except occasionally Mia asked for juice or some kind of cracker. A girl could live there for days.

Jack was there, in the kitchen, with a knife and she was at the table drinking wine. He pointed the knife at her and at himself. He gestured with the knife and he laughed. His skin covered him like a film of milk: she could see right into his bones. She kept sipping the wine. He was chopping mushrooms and complimenting her haircut. When he grabbed her wrist too firmly, she did not stop him. She wanted the pain to continue on beyond the outline of her body, past the windows and into the yard and all the way to the edge of what she considered her life.

On the news, they said the man had kept them in the basement behind the locked orange door for up to two weeks, one girl at a time. Inside, he had wire and metal. Elaine imagined a large drain in the middle of the floor and lots of cement. She compiled this image from television reports and a detective show she watched once. She invented horrific images of rope burns on wrists and small bruises just beginning to rise on inner thighs or the tender skin just beneath the armpit. When she closed her eyes, she saw the color of ripe plums and the yellow of a tornado sky.

She wanted to explain the situation to him. "Jack," she would say. "Mia's gone." He knew that. Mia's chair was empty at the dinner table and her bed remained neat. But still her pillow smelled of honeydew and lemons. The quilts were stale. Elaine could no longer lie on the bed and sleep. She used to. Before, she could lie on the bed listening to Jack breathe deeply in the other room. She would fall asleep and wake up alone. How did it happen a child created her own space, a curved hollow, and then occupied it? But when she disappeared the space remained, so that that there was always a place to which she could return.

At the grocery store near her house, Elaine stood transfixed in the magazine aisle. She found one entitled *True Crime* with articles about missing girls and men who were doing life in prison. Even the glossy women's magazines had articles about the missing girls or girls who had escaped and what they were doing now. They were filled with photographs displaying the beauty of each girl. While she was standing there, a man came up beside her and started looking through the magazines, finally picking up a *Seventeen*. Elaine turned to look at him. She studied his profile. If she ever had to ID him in a lineup, she decided she could. She had watched such things on cop shows, and she knew how to focus in on an identifying feature. She memorized the way his graying hair curled around his ear, and the slight raise in his nose around the bridge. Medium height, she thought. About the same weight as Jack. The man turned to her and forced a smile. He turned back to his magazine uncomfortably. "That's not yours," said Elaine, and snatched the magazine out of his hands. She walked away from him slowly, turning back to look at him once, reassuring herself that he saw the way she was looking at him.

Jack had never worried about anything. He leaned back in his recliner and smiled, sipping beer, humming. He never considered that the news might be speaking of him. "Warning! Danger." Sometimes Elaine wanted to slap him and sometimes she did.

The reporters called her courageous, the way she sat straight up in court, her black cardigan snug around her shoulders, how she looked him right in the eye and said it. Elaine tried not to hate her for being so beautifully alive, her white skin glowing on the TV, her blonde hair radiating. Elaine's bones ached. She studied the black frame of the TV set and the way the girl looked frozen there: alive and shiny.

Jack was gone now too, but his voice remained. It appeared, several times a day, through windows or on the answering machine. Sometimes she saw his body and his face through the screen door. Only an arm's length separated them. If she reached out her hand, she might touch him. But he might disappear too. Crumble, only an image that she had invented.

The woman next door screamed with what Elaine considered *fierce anguish*. She yelled words Elaine had not heard or thought in years. The woman screamed at her young daughter and Elaine had to stop herself from dashing outside and screaming back. In the middle of the night, when Elaine heard the woman's yowling, she forced her fingernails into the palm of her own hand. When she felt the blood rising off her skin in small drops, she rolled over and closed her eyes again.

She was just trying to watch some mindless TV, get her mind off things, and there she was, a thin blonde wearing a tiny t-shirt and tight black shorts, demonstrating a home exercise machine. Elaine imagined the cables wrapped around the girl's neck, the raw, red bruise the force would leave. She gasped. The blonde girl smiled and continued to pull the weights down toward herself. And then Elaine started to cry, sob really. She would have to admit to herself later that she was sobbing when she heard the knock on the front door.

"Jack," she said. "You have to stay away." He'd come back for a shirt, or a certain book. "Take everything," she said. "Except the TV." "Maybe you shouldn't watch the news," he said. "I know it upsets you." "What upsets me," she said, "is the existence of happiness. And smiles. I don't like the way they smile."

Elaine looked for the man behind closed doors. He could have been in the closet or the laundry room or in the basement. There were no doors she had not opened but now she began to wonder if the doors she thought she knew led to unseen rooms and forgotten cells.

"How could you?" she was saying to the criminal's wife. "You have children of your own." The wife had not done anything, the news reported, but ignore the large door and whatever was behind it. When they showed the door, it was bound with a chain and a padlock. Elaine could picture the door perfectly: a large metal apparatus, painted orange, with a large handle, like the door to a meat locker or deep freeze. How could you? Elaine thought.

*Jet,* Jack's note said, *I need to figure out what the quiet means.* He only called her by her nickname now, as if she were diminishing. Then he came by only once in awhile for a forgotten shirt or to pick up mail. But he might come by and knock and Elaine would sit on the basement steps, crying quietly and biting her lip, letting the blood pool in the bottom of her mouth. "Jet," he would say through the screen door. She imagined what his face might look like: a pixilated newspaper photograph, grainy in the distance.

The girl next door had a name that started with M, Melissa or Maggie. Elaine was sure she was the one who left the basket of flowers on the doorstep, but she doesn't know when. Now she hides in the living room dark and peers between the blinds. She likes to watch the girl walk home from school. To be sure someone sees her.

The room with the orange door was just an old basement recreation room that he had converted into a safe of sorts. He installed a lock and had only one key made, which he kept in his wallet and hid in various places around the house at night. Inside the room were ropes and wires and a bed made out of metal with loops on the four corners where ropes could be attached. Next to the bed was a small cage; it looked about the size of a kennel for a medium-sized dog. It had a lock on it. Why did they have to show that on the news?

Elaine had her scissors on the nightstand and pushpins next to the scissors, and tape and string. There were more girls every day, and their faces began to blur together. Becky, Stephanie, Lauren, Jenny. She could name them all. There's a man, she thought. She couldn't imagine a woman taking the small, soft hand of a girl and leading her down those basement stairs. Why would a woman do that? Women did far worse things, just by opening their arms and offering what passed for comfort.

The pictures lodged in her mind like slivers. She couldn't extract them. Once she had seen them, they lived there forever.

Here was a photograph of Mia at age five. If Elaine held her thumb over the face, the body could belong to anyone. Mia was wearing her favorite white dress, with lace up near the neck. There was pink ribbon and the shoes shone in the white light. Behind Mia was darkness, a background reduced to nothing by the negative which registered only extremes: black or white.

He knocked and she ignored his voice. She felt safe in the dark, as if she were listening for something. What was it?

There had been a picnic once, the three of them, a family, and a blanket. They sat in a lopsided circle, the food in the middle. Mia was only eating fruit then, cantaloupe, watermelon, berries. Jack kept offering her crackers, cheese, sandwiches. Even though they formed a circle, Elaine thought of Mia as separate, her own universe, with rules that only applied to her. She thought that together she and Jack exerted a kind of gravity that kept Mia close. Close, but not in the same galaxy. They could observe her galaxy but not inhabit it. That's what mothering felt like to her.

She left the door unlocked now, and remained in the basement. She had the remnants of an old kitchen and she used the electric kettle to make herself tea. The music of mice in the walls did nothing to disturb her routine.

Once, if someone had asked her to choose, she could have chosen. Take Jack, she'd have said. A girl can live without a father, but not a mother. Take Jack. Now she would say, take me.

Where had the smell of lilacs gone? Through the basement windows she could see crocuses forcing their way through the dirt, their cheerful blooms arguing for something, only she couldn't recall what.

"Jet," he said. "Jet?" He had taken to knocking on the basement windows now, so that she had to lie perfectly still.

If Elaine could keep one photograph of their family the way it was, it wouldn't be the portrait of them at the park, with trees in the background. It would be the photograph Mia took on the same day which shows only part of Mia's leg and Elaine's arm and the side of Jack's face. There's blue sky in the background and everyone is fuzzy, as if an outside force was pulling them in opposite directions, but so slowly that no one could tell.

Behind the door, there were white sheets and pillows and stuffed animals, all the things young girls like. Ruby curtains. Dried blood, she thought, and then tried to take it back. But she couldn't. Once she had seen the picture of it, the words rose up. When she closed her eyes, her skin began to slip from her bones.

When the downstairs grew colder, she burrowed under the blankets like a gerbil. When Mia's gerbil had babies, Elaine had to take them away. "Why?" asked Mia. Elaine thought perhaps Mia would cry, so she had made up a story about how the babies needed air and space in order to get bigger and bigger. Elaine had eventually given away the babies to a family who had a daughter who wanted gerbils. Elaine never told Mia the truth: mother gerbils eat their babies.

The knocking woke her up. Someone was at the back door, just at the top of the basement stairs. Was he saying Jet? Or help? In her dream, the voice had been Mia's and behind the plea for help had been a man's voice, low and threatening. Elaine could still feel the rope, burning around her wrists.

"Jet," the voice said again. "Where's Mia?"

"That's how it is with outer space," Mia had told her once. "It only looks like it goes on forever. But there's a wall there. See?

It's painted blue, like the sky. And then I'll be blue, right? Part of space."

Elaine would say that the voice had been the man's, though she had never actually heard his voice. Mia told me, she said, which caused people to gasp and hide their mouths behind their hands. Jack had reached out an arm, which Elaine swatted away. When she thought of another person's skin touching hers, she had to rush into the bathroom and close the door. She never thought about what had happened next.

The girl next door disappeared. Or at least Elaine stopped seeing her, which amounted to the same thing. What good was it to be alive if no one ever saw you? Elaine thought about this as she pulled the afghan around her legs. The view through the windows was dark now, full of dirt and clouds.

If only she had seen her. If only she had a picture of Mia, slightly turning to catch one last glimpse of her mother. Her hair slightly in front of her eyes, her right arm pulling her backwards, while her left arm reached out toward Elaine. She had her own specific gravity and Elaine would get sucked right in. But she hadn't seen her. It had all happened without Elaine knowing or suspecting the least thing. She hadn't felt a twinge in her gut, she hadn't even sensed the slightest problem.

Jack had loved her. He held her in his arms, squeezing tight, tighter. She had liked it. He had pushed her wrists up, holding them down with his hands. She had liked that too. There were pictures of such things on the TV. But she couldn't stand the sounds, like cries of pain. She watched everything on mute.

Elaine looked in the mirror. The eyes were place holders for something, an idea, vague but sharp-edged and dangerous. She kept looking, hoping for an emotion approaching recognition. The woman who stared back looked familiar, like someone she had once seen on TV.

# Dioramas Of The Domestic Landscape

## Window #4

Some rooms are like beverages, beer, say, or coffee. Other rooms are weather: a sunny, cloudless expanse or a dreary, rain-soaked Monday. This room is the latter, though the walls are a pleasant-enough brown. A thin layer of beige paint covers the floor, approximating carpet, or perhaps wood. There are no windows, no attempt even at windows, so that the interior is dark, despite the light that shines in when the top is removed. The room is vacant, and does not appear to ever have been inhabited. The lack of inhabitants is palpable, and fills the room. A tiny chair, made of toothpicks sloppily glued together, waits in the corner. A desk sits against the far wall, but it is empty, no paper, no pens. The room is expectant, a canvas waiting for the first drop of paint, a gesture, anything that will demonstrate, finally, meaning.

# Bitter On The Tongue

That was back in Seattle, in the days of studio apartments and Rock Hoppers, twelve-day backpacking trips with guides named Dude and Dude Two.

Once I invented a whole town of Daves and they all had horrible skin diseases—Dave was actually my boyfriend once—and the whole beer thing—I mean, it's not like I live in a Raymond Carver story, it was good beer—the beer was just a fringe benefit.

That was when I met him, let's call him Dave as well, why not? They were all Dave in their way: short, underweight, leveled by a single imperative.

Dave the brewer, Dave the mountain man, Dave's presence in my life was circumscribed, shall we say, by events out of his control.

*So maybe this is it, maybe not?*

A man like him and a woman like me, we were like two trains leaving from two separate stations at two different times, headed in two different directions.

Those were the days of Tori and ani, endless blue days, inside at least, while outside it poured a seamless gray.

He was a lot of things besides short: smart, sure smart, witty, and nice. Maybe too nice, nice in a way that makes your teeth ache, that glossy, just too nice.

He, of course, blamed himself, as if I were some mountain he had failed to conquer, as if he had seen me from afar, the way we often looked at the Cascades and believed we knew all about them because we could see them, their jagged peaks and never-melting snow packs.

The mountain bike I can do without, but I miss the studio apartment with the bay window and the built-in bookcases where I could go for days with no one knocking on my door.

A decent cup of coffee is not negotiable, not in Seattle, the so-called birthplace of the American espresso bar, the home of the Pile Driver, and not being able to make a decent cup of coffee is a deal breaker.

The night was flannel, a soft gray that moved in around us as the sun set and the stars emerged, little forest fires, burning, one by one, in the distance.

Dave couldn't brew a decent cup of coffee.

He told me that he liked to watch me, early in the morning, from a distance.

He'd come over to my apartment and take off his shoes, then pretty soon his socks would be off and he'd leave little sweaty footprints on my hardwood floors, so I had to make him leave before he took off his hat or, god help me, his coat or his shirt.

He was short, skinny and short.

He had his own backpacking equipment and he worked at a microbrewery.

He was so underweight, he was like a tadpole you could see through, see the veins and everything, and the little tadpole heart pushing orange blood through those little tadpole veins.

You know how it is, you wake up in the morning, freezing, bleary eyed, tired, maybe hung over, and all you want is coffee, and there he is, huddled next to the fire with his two-hundred-dollar backpacking espresso maker steaming the powdered milk into a cloudy froth, and he pours it into a mug half filled with what you can only describe, kindly, as water that looks as if it has been stirred with a brown crayon.

He'd watch me counting the loaves, arranging them on the shelves, flirting with the grocery stockers, the whole time studying my behavior, studying me as if I were some kind of indigenous life-form, some kind of representative sample.

Dave! Stop calling me!

Our relationship consisted of things to do without taking off our shirts, things to do wearing many layers, outdoor things, like carrying really heavy stuff on our backs as we scaled steep mountains and wielded ice picks.

I was the woman who delivered bread, the woman who wouldn't let him take off his coat, the woman who needed coffee, the woman who loved the interior of her studio apartment, the woman who loved living alone.

We didn't have a problem with who was in charge and who was taken care of.

I could smell the grass growing dewy and heavy, the wet smell moving up toward us like fog.

I couldn't drink it, could I?

Another favorite activity involved weight lifting and cigarettes.

Marriage is not about bone structure.

He wanted to be the hero who saved everyone, the guides, the Sherpas, the society dame. Me.

We were standing on my deck, a long porch that I shared with all the apartments on the second floor, and we heard the couple next door fighting. He called her a bitch and she threw something that shattered, making a glassy sound, both beautiful and sad, like the last note of a song.

I was something rotten and tasteless, bitter on the tongue.

*I'll see you soon.*

He had the nicest collarbone I'd ever seen.

He was a drug, not like aspirin, not a useful drug, but sugar or caffeine. I was addicted, I needed the drug, but I didn't love him. I didn't love the drug. I loved the feeling of running my tongue over the residue on my teeth.

And this is it. The ever after that, happily or not, lives on.

# Dioramas Of The Domestic Landscape

## Window #5

Certainly all the appliances are miniature, but they behave normally, opening to reveal their gleaming contents. The dishwasher door raises and lowers, though the dishes inside cannot be removed, and the dishwasher performs no actual function. But see how it shines and reflects back the frozen faces of the family? In this kitchen, all the fruits and vegetables are glued in place. None of these apples will rot, attracting fruit flies, and the bounty in the refrigerator will never grow old. See how the mother smiles, standing at the counter, offering plastic cookies to her hungry and eager offspring? She is red, but her children are blue, and her son seems to have a baseball bat slung over his shoulder. Though the cupboards overflow, the children need no sustenance. The shining tile floor never dirties, the kitchen towels never need laundering. Where is the husband? Outside, of course, for we can not see him here.

# After: Crime Scene

In the photo, you can't see the silence, but the house sits angrily and clenches. Before, the noise rose singularly and then fell away, the same way a person falls, the way a knife divides, flesh from flesh, before from after, a woman from her self. You can't see how the body lay, eyes open, watching. The cries drifted to the ceiling. Now they hang heavy in the curtains, like smoke. See how the whole room is about to sink? Like a mind, the quiet waits, thinking. The room moves like blood into white cloth, seeping. Like fingers in search of sight.

# Knives In The Kitchen

The kitchen store dictates a certain level of domesticity: I want to acquire the right garlic press, the correct culinary attitude, the perfect knife for the job.

*Serrated: for delicately slicing cakes or bread*

Nothing in the kitchen rises to the occasion. All implements must be coerced into taking their parts, speaking their correct lines, eliciting the correct response: awe, dismay, pain.

*Utility: for everyday kitchen jobs*

I understand the angry teeth of the bread knife. I pick it up and saw the loaf with an earnest intensity. I eat the crusty heel out of spite.

*Chef: for chopping, mincing and dicing*

No one worries about sounds from the kitchen: there are so many things to go wrong, liquids boiling over, sauces adhering to the incorrect surfaces, misjudgments that result in blood spilling forth, over the cutting board and down, onto the floor.

*Boning: for separating meat from bone*

I gasp, spying the gash in my hand, where the thumb begins its bony travel to the wrist. I'd been holding a lamb chop at just the wrong angle. I start to feel the pain, but I admire my handiwork, the fluidity of my stroke.

*When using a knife, pay attention.*

If I were a chef, my approach would be different. But as it is, any knife will do. It is amazing the tools that can be adapted to serve our purposes, like the marsupial who uses her pouch to tote sticks back to the breeding ground. As far as I know, this has never happened.

*Carving: for dividing the bounty into consumable portions*

A small knife might be concealed, easily, in the palm of one's hand. A larger knife, up in the sleeve. In summer, one must be more clever about how one transports sharp implements, using towels, shirts, pockets, for such endeavors. Certain knives were made with the sole intention of concealment. But what's the challenge in that?

*Carry knives properly.*

When purchasing a knife at an upscale kitchen store, no one eyes you with suspicion, wondering what you might use it for. "This one is fantastic!" the clerk said. She began to list the recipes in which I might enlist the assistance of this tool. "And it stays sharp forever." She wrapped the knife in brown paper and slid it into a bag. I thanked her for her assistance.

*Don't put knives in a sink, or anywhere they cannot be seen.*

There is a certain satisfaction in the heft of an expensive tool. When the blade comes down, rhythmically, mechanically, ignorant of what it does but performing nonetheless, continuing to slice, sliver, dice, it's like the slam of a door, repeatedly, at the will of a strong hand.

*Cut away from the body.*

There is a particular equanimity inherent in knives. No job outweighs the next or the previous. The knife is the perfect beard, remembering nothing, foretelling nothing, conveying nothing, except in the evenness with which it carries out its duties.

*Paring: for trimming away the excess*

A person might grip you by the wrist, too tightly, but you grasp a knife, a concept you can manipulate to your liking. The side of a chef's knife, for example, can be used to smash garlic in order to easily remove the skin. The handle of a knife, then, might be used on a person's head. But there is always the business end of the knife as well.

*Keep knives sharp.*

The business of sharpening knives can induce a trancelike state. The pulling, quickly and decisively, of the blade across the steel shaft, has the ring of music, the tone of a prayer bell singing out its koan.

*Steak: for a specific cut of meat*

Here he is now, in the kitchen. He's disturbing the perfect alignment of objects. Too many cooks, they say, though there is no cooking here, only the way stainless steel vibrates when it begins to move toward the object of its affection.

*Use knives only for cutting.*

If it had happened in the garage, it could have been a wrench, or the car itself. Each space has its apparatus, and we who observe can readily discern the plot about to unfold by simply observing the elements in their alignment. A butcher block full of knives, each sheathed in its slot, anticipating its fate, the one job for which it is suited, can indicate the impending events if only we stop to catalog each detail, how the paring knife perches on the edge of my vision, how the chef's knife calls out to me, so that I can hear the thump, thump of its blade, how the bread knife beckons like a shark with its mouth closed.

*Use the correct knife for the job.*

You can't force it. You can't cut a tomato with a cheese knife. When you feel the knife in your hand, you know what's correct. The heft of the steel and graphite, the single piece that fits the blade, squarely, into the hilt. You have to wait for the job to come to you. Eventually it will. You hear footsteps, events approaching you, establishing the future and the past in just this moment. The knife is patient, without anticipation or fear. The knife waits, deaf and dumb, as the flesh draws near.

# The Third Suspect

In every marriage, there is always a third suspect to which all evidence can be matched. If you followed the story, you remember the confusion between *surgical implement* and *tool*.

The blood congeals into an amoeba, a virus—the brief spots are constellations, dot-to-dots spelling out *unhappiness, inexplicable, motive*. There is a range of possibility indicated by the DNA patterns which excludes *within*. But it does not exclude *other woman, stranger, handyman, neighbor*. It does not exclude *now*.

Forty years later, questions still circulate. A woman changes in that time—her skin shrinking back from the facts. A man ages and a child thinks adulterous thoughts, thinks *other man, mailman, doctor*.

But this is the shape of footprints, the blows made by blunt objects, the array of wounds. This is what jurisprudence cannot erase. In my mind, there are flames. I invent equivocation. Justice is abstract, a pool of blood beside the bed.

In the end, everyone dies: the father, the suspect, the marriage. Eventually, the child.

# Miss America: A Story In Sestinas

I.

Miss America sang at my parents' wedding, though singing was not her crown-winning talent. Miss America, this particular Miss America, Miss America 1965, was my mother's best friend from high school and besides that a ventriloquist, meaning she held a doll on her knee and by not moving her lips made everyone believe it talked. But at the time Miss America sang at my parents' wedding she was not, actually, Miss America, but rather Miss Dallas well on her way to becoming Miss Texas and then, finally and unpredictably, Miss America. She was the only Miss America to be voted, by her fellow contestants and before she won the crown, Miss Congeniality. But that's not how she came to have the same name as my sister. Or, should I say, that's not how my sister came to be named Miss America, or, more accurately, Lynda Kay MacMurtry Miller; I blame that on my mother.

As the pageant was being televised, I wandered around the house looking for my mother. I usually could find her, even when she was hiding in the shower trying not to breathe—I considered it, and still do, a talent. On this particular evening, my mother suffered from what I came to refer to as Lynda sickness, or nausea brought on by the presence of my sister. When I found my mother pressing her pale cheek against the closed lid of the toilet, I started to tell her, but she put up her hand and said, "Not now. I can't talk." "Boy," I remember saying, "aren't you Miss Congeniality. You don't even care that Linda Kay just won Miss America."

The next day the headline read "Local girl wins the heart and crown of America." I was sitting at the kitchen table, next to my mother. She read aloud from the paper, "Linda Kay MacMurtry is the first Miss America to also be voted Miss Congeniality." My mother sighed deeply, which, at six months pregnant, was rapidly becoming her only talent. "Hey," I said, running my hand along her forearm, "wanna talk?" She sighed and got up from the table to phone her sister.

Three months later, I was at the hospital for the birth of my very own sister. "I know you don't like the idea," my mom said as they wheeled her down the hall, "but I'm naming her after Miss America." "After it's born," I replied, "then we'll talk." I watched as the hallway leading to the delivery room swallowed up my mother. I began whistling, Buddy Holly I think it was, another of my particular talents. I kept whistling, hoping for a boy, musing on the meaning of the word *congenial*.

Sure, it's easy enough now to say I was no Miss Congeniality. But let's face it, neither was my sister. I know it's not her fault that she was named after Miss America, but I also know that being born doesn't count as a talent. I mean, we both knew neither of us was destined to be famous, like, say, Miss America. But try telling that to my mother. That is, if you could get her to stop planning and fussing long enough so that you could actually talk.

Here's the usual "talk." My mom, wearing coral lipstick and a blouse best described by the word "blouse," would sit my sister down and lecture, beginning—let's not act surprised here—with congeniality. My sister, yeah, Lynda, would smile and nod benignly at my mother. My mother would smile and nod benignly at my sister. Then the talk would turn to Miss America. And then she'd arrive at the problem of talent.

After mom's lectures there was no talking to my sister. Her head was full of swimsuit competitions, evening gowns, congeniality, blah blah blah, Miss America. My mother always said, and here I am quoting directly, "I'm the one with the talent."

II.

Ninety percent of former Miss Americas have gone on to marry some kind of executive: movie, corporate, television. Very few Miss Americas have had a unique talent, except Linda the Ventriloquist and a woman named Judith Ford who has the dubious honor of being the only trampolinist to win the crown. Well, let's not forget Miss America 1954 who recited a poem which she had never before spoken aloud—seriously, this is all true. Many Miss Americas had three names—Barbara Jo Walker, Sharon Kay Ritchie, Lynda Lee Mead—but only one, Kaye Lani Rae Rafko, had four. My sister, if she had won the crown (and if she had been married at the time and had added her husband's name to her own), could have been the first five name Miss America. But don't tell my mother.

We tried to find Lynda a talent, and no one tried harder than my mother. "I know," she said, "she can do endorsements—we can get her on television." "That's not a talent, Ma, not according to 'Miss America.'" Since the time Lynda was born, no, since the first Linda became Miss America, my mother has been obsessed with the crown. "Mom," I'd ask, "what are you doing this for?" But no matter what answer she gave, we both knew it wasn't true.

Everything I say about my sister is true. Here's one thing even she wouldn't deny: she's exactly like our mother. Right down to the number of martinis they each have to drink before spilling their secrets, crying, then passing out on the floor: four. Nowadays I let them sleep in the kitchen, their legs splayed out at pornographic angles, while I watch some TV. Sometimes, out of some need for revenge or a love of irony, I slip in the documentary *The Road to the Crown*. Even now we can't get through one day without one of us saying it: *Miss America.*

When she started junior high, Lynda cried every day about being named after a former Miss America. "Whatever they are saying about you or the first Linda Kay, honey," my mom would repeat, "it just isn't true." Then she would intone some general truisms about the road being rocky and wouldn't Lynda show them when she was waving from Atlantic City after being crowned. Lynda would continue sobbing and cry out, "Oh mother!" Since we had just gotten cable, I pretended to watch television. This happened every day at four.

My mother had been shopping Lynda around to the various pageants since she was three or four. "This is how it goes," my mother would say when Lynda pouted, "not everyone gets to be Miss America." Because I was older, I could stay home alone and "do homework" my mother said, but usually I'd invite some neighbor kids over to watch television. I told myself that was the only way we would ever learn the difference between what our parents said and what was true. "The only reality is the crown," said my mother. The fucking crown.

My sister was six when she won a kiddy crown. "Little Miss Metro" I think it was and I swear she beat out kids who were only four. "Oh, you're just jealous," said my mother. "You want to be Miss America." "Yeah," I said, "that's true." The truth was the only thing I wanted was a Miss-America-free-zone and my own television.

My mother prayed Lynda would be crowned Miss America. My sister prayed for my mother's prayers to come true. I prayed my mother, Miss America, anyone, would buy me a television.

III.

This is later, but before Lynda went into rehab and after my mother retired from her job with the Department of Corrections. Before Lynda got divorced and before I got involved with a marriage which ended, not surprisingly, in divorce. It's not unusual for two middle-aged daughters to go home to live with their mother. What is unusual is that one of them is named after a former Miss America and their mother's new roommate is said former Miss America. The complete story on how they came to cohabitate remains a secret, but I know for sure that it involved a bar. However, I wasn't going to let their postretirement antics interfere with my newfound career.

I awoke each morning at five a.m. to get started on my writing career. I began each day by reading through what I had written the previous day and, with a sharp pencil, writing in any corrections. Regardless of how any day started, each day ended at about two p.m. when I emerged from the shower, dabbed a bit of musk behind each ear, threw on a billowy dress and headed for the bar. As I said, this was before anyone in the house felt obliged to whisper when they said the word *divorce*. Not that my intention was to pick up men or to find someone to marry, but I sure wasn't going to spend the rest of my days, my increasingly more orgasmic days (according to *Cosmo*), with my mother and Miss America. Did I neglect to mention certain irritating habits of my mother?

Not that there are not hundreds of people more irritating than my mother. However, few people adopt the habit necessary to make irritation a career. Aside from slurping her coffee, insistently and without fail, and spending all her time in the kitchen just outside my door singing, as loud as she could, "Waltzing Matilda," my mom began and maintained the habit of addressing Lynda, both of them, as "Miss America." And she could not stand to be corrected. Linda Kay, the first one, came to my mother's house seeking refuge from divorce. Divorce, it turned out, was just what I was seeking in that bar.

I don't want to give the false impression that all I ever did was hang out in that bar. On the contrary, after my morning writing I would perform all sorts of menial errands in the company of my mother. My mother had refused to drive ever since, on the way home from one of those stupid pageants, she trashed a Cadillac she had gotten in one of her divorces. So chauffeuring my mother around became my second, unwanted, career. Which was fine, really, except for my mother's belated—"no! left! here! now!"—corrections. After a few of these trips, I realized I should have gone to the bar, or stayed home and left the driving to Miss America.

Just a word about the former Miss America. It turns out she used to frequent the very same bar. She took my mother there after they ran into each other at the Department of Corrections. Why the Department of Corrections I don't know, and I haven't been able to get much information out of my mother. Whatever it was, it has something to do with my mother's retirement from her short-lived Department of Corrections "career." And something to do with Miss America's impending, unfinished divorce.

Aside from religion, I remain unsure as to the reasons Miss America didn't go through with her divorce. It could be she didn't want to tarnish her reputation as Miss America. It could have something to do with her inspirational speaking career. But none of that stopped her from hanging out at the bar. Or from moving in with and sponging off my mother. Or ending my mother's career in corrections.

I can't blame my sister's divorce on the bar. I can't blame it on Miss America or my mother. I blame everything, including

my sister's failed rehab, on my attempted career, on my obsession with making corrections.

IV.

No one would blame me, it's true, for the fact my sister never became Miss America. I blame that on my sister's enormous lack of talent, if you exclude drinking. She's the one who first took me to the bar, a small, dimly lit shack specializing in margaritas, domestic beer, and nearsighted men. We never told my mother where we were going except to say "out" and that we'd be home "later" and not to wait up and please leave the door unlocked, please (as she had yet to trust either of us, again, with our own set of keys) please, mother. The main reason, besides my mother, that Lynda never became Miss America is her name, Lynda. Or perhaps that's being much too unfair and the main and only reason is a simple one: Lynda is dumb.

I only mean to be truthful when I say Lynda is dumb. Not that there isn't a long tradition of dumb in the history of Miss America. Just that she had her own brand of dumb which is forever associated in my mind with my sister, and I call this dumb "Lynda." For example, we are out drinking. Some nice, clean, and not-too-ugly men will buy us a round and the first thing Lynda does is start talking about our mother. Can you think of a simpler way of scaring off men?

And Lynda's brand of dumb is not restricted to men. If there is a situation that calls for cunning and intelligence, Lynda will respond with dumb. For example, our mother. She would go on and on about the importance of being Miss America. Lynda would respond with anger and violence, which is a sure sign, even in a twelve-year-old, of someone who would rather be drinking. But instead of keeping this inside, and continuing to nod benignly at our mother, Lynda would go off on some stupid tirade for which there is only one name: Lynda.

Here is my first clear memory of Lynda. In this memory, we are a family defined by the absence of men. On this particular night, a lightning storm lit our room and we could hear our mother down in the kitchen drinking. Lynda wanted to lean out our third-story window, topless, into the rainy night, but I admonished her, as was my way, by stating plainly "that's dumb." "If you do that," I said, thinking I was threatening her, "you'll ruin your chances of ever being Miss America." "If you don't," she replied, "you'll always live with Mom."

Something in this memory explains the way my sister and I aligned ourselves against our mother. My sister and I felt the same way about anyone being named Lynda. We agreed that she would never become, nor did she want to become, Miss America. We were curious, a curiosity we were sure our mother did not share, about the world of men. We were not convinced, as our mother seemed to be, that men were dumb. We sat quietly, listening to the clinking of ice in a solitary glass, the sound of drinking.

It was a comfort, the sounds of our mother's drinking. But, we realized, it was not a comfort to our mother. Lynda sat on the stairs every night, listening to the music of ice against glass, struck dumb. I sat at the top of the stairs, twirling the hem of my pajamas, studying Lynda. I was older, but I knew Lynda would precede me into the world of men. And I knew the reason: she was not Miss America.

From our mother, I learned a thing or two about drinking; so did Lynda. But what Lynda could not learn from our mother she would learn from men. But she could not learn how not to be dumb, or how to be better at not being Miss America.

## V.

But back to the bar. My sister enters first, pushing the door away from her as she flips her hair over her right shoulder, and I follow her in. Did I neglect to mention that my sister is beautiful? She does not take after our mother, or her absent and forgotten father, nor is she some fluke combination of their genes which resulted in her long, auburn hair and perfect (heroin-addict-looking) body. My sister is some kind of miracle, and by miracle I mean mistake. She looks nothing like me.

My sister never denied any association with me. Even when we were in the bar. A good-looking guy would come over and put his hand on her arm and when she introduced me as her sister, he would register that information as some kind of mistake. But he didn't understand that I was the one who decided which guys were in. They miscalculated and thought the brain was attached to the body. Or that I didn't hear each one of them as they clichéd in Lynda's ear, "you're beautiful."

So I first started going to the bar in the company of beauty. And then it was just me. Without Lynda, I felt alone in the bar, inside my head, inside my body. I got addicted to being alone and the only place I could be was at the bar. I'd walk there from Mom's house and look at my feet as I went in. Without Lynda I felt like I was sinning, but I also felt like a miracle, my own special brand of mistake.

"Are you alone, or am I mistaken?" He wasn't good at pickup lines, but he was beautiful. I slid over in the booth to let him in. I sipped my beer and let him look at me. "Wanna get out of this dark bar?" He ran his finger the length of my body.

Unlike Lynda, I am normally attracted to the mind of a man, not his body. However, in this case, paying sole attention to his body was not a mistake. I also, unlike Lynda, do not bring home men that I have just met in some bar. But, as I said, he was beautiful. And, for whatever reason, he liked me. And I didn't care if he had a wife, was a drunk, or what emotional state he was in.

Lynda kicked on my door, begging to be let in. She forced the lock, slamming against the door with the full weight of her body. When she saw him lying there, she just turned to go, hoarsely saying, "Excuse me. My mistake." Her eyes popped out, like she too could see he was beautiful. Either that or she knew him from the bar.

I told Lynda to stay in my room, but that might have been a big mistake. I couldn't have my mother rushing in, seeing his naked body, even if it was beautiful. I wanted to limit what my mother knew about me and the guy I brought home from the bar.

VI.

Belatedly, I had found Lynda's true talent: men. The one in bed with me, besides being a first-rate drinker, had married Lynda one night after he had won some money gambling and so they drove to Vegas. But let's not confuse marriage with love. This would be Lynda's first divorce, though they were not yet divorced when he sought me out, knowing that I was, in fact, the sister of a woman who would never become Miss America. My mother, on the other hand, was still blissfully ignorant of Lynda's true talent, and I intended to maintain her in that state of ignorance until her death. "Lynda," I screamed between my teeth. "Get him out of here." This was a scene we had played throughout her teenage years, the him in question always unquestionably hers.

I sent Lynda to rehab, for drinking and for men, but neither took. She returned home to sit at the kitchen table with my mother, Miss America and myself, a bottle of gin between us and the martini shaker being passed in a clockwise direction. Lynda still frequented the bar, but I stayed home with my corrections. Miss America had insomnia and many nights would join me on the couch for *Wild Kingdom* or something tasteless on the Playboy Channel.

Sitting next to the original Linda, who had not aged well and had taken up smoking when she realized she was going to outlive her 401K, I often felt that perhaps my sister was aptly named and that my mother had always known something about the original Linda that she had never shared. One night, after a few particularly strong martinis, I got out my sister's kiddy crown and put it on her, affixing it with bobby pins to her fading auburn hair. The original Linda, her voice deepened by cigarettes, lifted a swizzle stick and began singing into it, in the manner of Bert Parks, "There She Is, Miss America."

Lynda, finally crowned, stood up and did a turn around the kitchen, waving her arm like a real professional, at us, her adoring fans.

# Dioramas Of The Domestic Landscape

## Window #6

It's just a bed. But this one is made of paper towels, many paper towels, folded and taped, maybe glued. Then a piece of fabric, flowery and blue, laid on top of the paper towel mattress and on top of that a small square of fleece. You can see the fuzz and almost feel the warmth, though the entire bed would hardly contain your thumb. There is a woman in this one, made from a clothespin, the old-fashioned kind with a rounded top that almost looks like a head. But she has two tiny beads for eyes, black, and a small dot of paint for a nose, pink. She has no mouth. Her dress is a rectangle of felt wrapped around the clothespin. But there are two lumps on her to approximate breasts and her arms, made of checkered fabric, cradle a baby. The woman stands between the bed and a crib, assembled from coffee stirrers and with a blanket the size of a postage stamp. The baby is just a wad of cloth curved and jammed together. There's no real baby. But the woman wants it to be a baby, and so it is. You can tell by the way she holds it. The round lump near the woman's breast is the baby's mouth. He wants to feed. The baby is a boy because the fabric is blue. The rest of the room is neutral, cardboard colored and drab. The woman has made some curtains, of the same fabric as her arms, which hang in squares around the room. But they don't cover windows. They cover closed squares the same texture as the floor.

# Temptations

An electrician stops by to look at her wiring. "You've got an old panel here," he says, slapping her circuit breaker. She tries to read sexual innuendo into everything, but it just isn't working.

*I like someone* reads one email she receives. *Can you guess who it is?*

A man in the supermarket: she imagines his soft lips against her collarbone. She avoids eye contact.

What is the nature of the conjugal contract? Two people agree to pool their money and their desire, or at least the enactment of their desire. The imagination is completely off-limits. The lust that dare not speak its name: that of a woman for the anonymous anatomy of a stranger.

Jimmy Carter said, "I've committed adultery in my heart many times."

While he speaks she tries not to imagine his penis in her mouth, his eyes rolling back, the dull thrum of his moaning. What is he saying? Something about the washing machine? Oh yeah, something about the traveling habits of contemporary families. God, she could die of boredom.

Not every man is attractive. That man there, for instance. Here she is, just exercising, sweaty, hair plastered to her forehead. But if he looked at her and smiled, she could become interested.

When was the last time she had a crush? When she thinks *crush* she feels the terrible weight of a man's body, the suffocation and thrill, the anticipation of satisfaction, a tickle on the roof of her mouth. The word is a tongue between her teeth. Not hers.

She remembers one man: his hair completely white, though he couldn't have been over forty. He was with his wife and they were buying novels. She smiled and complimented him on his glasses. His eyes were an intense blue. She thought the wife smirked as they turned away from her.

She called a man to come over and fix her phone. But they sent a woman.

She finds reading most thrilling of all, hoping the author will maneuver the characters into a bedroom, or a room with a couch or a big overstuffed chair. She remembers a boyfriend pursuing her over the back of the couch and onto the floor. She has to stop reading for a moment. Whatever happened to him?

Her husband gets a haircut and buys a suit for his job interview. When he arrives home and opens the door, she experiences amnesia. This guy is okay, she thinks. Who is he?

# Dioramas Of The Domestic Landscape

## Window #7

There is no bathroom, so we just have to assume that the wooden people do not need one. A bathroom might provide the opportunity for displays of fluffy towels, shiny colorful tiles, and bloody pieces of cotton. Bathroom color schemes are difficult and could be displayed through contrast, but as we have no example of that here we will pass on to the next exhibit.

# Domestic Drama

He finds me in the bedroom. I have the butcher knife and I'm holding it in my right hand and with my left I'm looking through a pile of clean laundry on the bed. I'm looking for a red handkerchief which I gave him for his last birthday and which would make a good tool for wiping up blood, but that's not why I'm looking for it. I'm looking for it because it had just sprung to my mind as I was deboning the chops for dinner. I hadn't seen it in months, and I thought that maybe it was missing or, I thought, maybe it was in the pile of clean clothes on the bed. That was the only place it could be. I had done all the laundry, the laundry room was clean, empty except for some dirty washcloths which could wait until next weekend.

I'm standing there with the knife in one hand and with the other expertly sorting the laundry into mine, his, and theirs, theirs being the kids, which they could deal with later when they got home from the various activities in which they were engaged. And then he comes in, accusingly, with his feet making loud noises in the hallway to announce his approach, and the way he stands there says what he wants to say, the way he fills up the doorway, his head almost touching the top and his shoulders about equidistant from each jamb, and he looks like a poster I once saw for a B movie, I forget the name, but he looks like the villain. All he lacks is the black fedora and a pug-nosed gun. But his face is like that, his nose aimed at me, and he says, "What are you doing?"

I'm sure he knows what I'm doing, that he has done something with the handkerchief, but he also could be referring to the fact that I hold a knife in one hand and the other is buried in clean clothes that smell of spring breezes or lilacs or fresh herbs or something. At an expensive boutique, I saw a bottle of fragrance called "Fresh Linen" and it wasn't clear to me if it was something you were supposed to spray on your linen or if it was something you were supposed to spray somewhere else, say in your bedroom, to make it smell like fresh linen, but that's what I think of when I look up and see him there, like a murderer or a detective, in the doorway. I think first of fresh linen and second of the butcher knife in my other hand. I might say, "Oh, nothing," and go on nonchalantly, except for the butcher knife. I had been using it to remove bones from lamb chops, which I remember are oozing on a cutting board in the kitchen. I think of them, just lying there leaking blood out into the white cutting board the way a red handkerchief might bleed dye into a load of all white clothes, socks, say, or men's underwear. As I think of this, I raise the butcher knife and I jab the end toward him, not at him exactly, as I'm sure he would claim, but just in his general direction. And I say something like "the red handkerchief, where is it?" I can see how someone who didn't know me might find the sight of the knife jarring, but I can't understand how someone like him, I mean we've been married for fourteen years, ever since we found out I was pregnant, how someone like him could perceive that gesture, the jab, how he could see that as threatening. I mean, I've never once in our whole marriage done anything like that. I'm just thinking of the lamb chops and the handkerchief and the laundry and I just want to know, where is it? Because I can't stand it when something is lost. I might not think about it for days, weeks even, but then when I remember it I can't think of anything else until it's found. So that's how it starts, innocently enough, I'm just looking for the handkerchief. With a butcher knife in one hand.

And then he says, "What handkerchief?" I mean really, what handkerchief? He had made such a big deal of it when he unwrapped it, how it would go so well with such and such a suit, and how he would be a bit of a dandy, with a handkerchief in his pocket, jutting out like some kind of sculpture. He quite liked it, and he may deny it now, but he made a big to-do over it. I'm sure the kids will remember, because they bought him a book or something and the red handkerchief overshadowed it. I do remember that he stood in front of the big plate-glass window, the one that overlooks the yard, he stood in front of that window with the handkerchief in his shirt pocket, and he had the book open like he was reading it. I remember now, it was a book about painters, like Romantic Painters or Painters of the Renaissance or something. And he had the book open and balanced on his hand, and he put the other on his chin to mime thinking. And the kids thought it great fun, and they cheered and took a picture. So he did like the book, of course, but it was the handkerchief that really completed the look, that really made him feel like he was lord of the manor, so to speak, king in his castle and whatnot. So that's why the handkerchief was so important when I suddenly thought of it as I was cutting through the meat. And then for him to pretend that he doesn't know what I'm talking about, well, it's preposterous. I mean, he goes to the trouble of posing for some kind of portrait painting, and then he pretends to forget it. Really. The man can be so infuriating. So when he asks me what I'm doing and then pretends not to know the item to which I'm referring… Well. He says that, he says, "I do not recall the item to which you are referring," as if I'm some dopey prosecutor who has just stumbled into his office, glad to be offered the job of licking his shoes. So that's when I realize that not only does he know the item to which I am referring, which he obviously does, but that he is hiding it for some reason.

See, lawyers think they can cover things over, as if they were magicians or conjurers. Remember that movie where the whole time the hero, who was he, one of those dark-eyed mysterious movie stars, he thinks he's conning everyone, and in the end, he's the one who's being conned? What's that film? In any case, exactly. He's making statements and asking questions like this is some kind of investigation, and the whole time his eyes dart back and forth exactly like that movie villain. So he seems likes he's the one asking the questions, but the whole time he's looking for an escape route, like I'm the one who's threatening him, like I'm the one who up and hid the red handkerchief. And why would he do that?

Well, that's when it comes to me, about the handkerchief being perfect for wiping up blood. I mean, where is it? If he used it, for example, to staunch his own blood, wouldn't it be in the dirty clothes? Wouldn't I stumble across it during my duties? Where else could it be? I always go through his pockets, so if it were there, I would have found it. But it wasn't there. So where was it? Exactly. Right.

So he comes in and starts asking me questions. And then he acts like he doesn't know. It is a butcher knife, and it is a simple jab, a gesture, like pointing with your finger, only I don't have a finger, I have a knife. So, it could be perceived as threatening. But I'm his wife. He backs slowly out into the hallway, as if I am a stranger with a switchblade. But I'm not. And I'm not threatening him. I'm merely gesturing. But where's the handkerchief? He still doesn't say. He's still proclaiming his innocence. And then the blood comes to me, you know, an image. Perhaps that's why I thought of it while I was cutting the meat, because the handkerchief resembles blood. I think it's crimson, technically. That's blood, right? So I'm looking at the blood, and I think of the handkerchief. Then, I'm looking at my husband, and I remember the blood.

"The chops," I say. Maybe I wave the knife a little. A little. And so I keep walking toward him, back to the kitchen, and he's backing up.

"No," he's saying. "No." And maybe I'm waving the knife, like what? I mean, I don't know. I have the knife, but I'm thinking about the chops, and how they are warming up and I have to get them back into the refrigerator. And I have to find the handkerchief, of course, because where is it? Things don't just disappear, everyone knows that. If you lose something, it still is somewhere, wherever you lost it. But a grown man doesn't just lose something precious to him. A gift from his wife. That's something that he keeps track of, something that he puts back in his drawer at the end of the day. I know, because I've seen him do it. He takes it out of his pocket and refolds it and puts in his top drawer. And then the change goes on the top of the dresser and so on. But the handkerchief always goes back in the top drawer. And I should know, but I haven't seen it in, what, weeks?

We're back in the kitchen. He sits down at the bar and watches me. I have the knife still, of course, and now I'm finishing with the chops. You have to do things that way, first one thing, and then the next. So I need to finish. You make the marinade, then you remove the bones, and then you put it all together. That's the way it's done. Things are done that way, step by step. So I have the knife and I'm working on the meat.

"Oh," he says, like he just realized. Like, oh, the knife is for cutting meat, like he finally understands the invention of knives, something he's never understood his whole life. And to tell you the truth, I don't like him in the kitchen with me. It's my place. I make the food, and I know where everything is, a place for everything. Things do not go missing in the kitchen. I know where my knives are, for example, and where the dish towels are and the measuring spoons, and so on. So him sitting here, it's like he's saying, I'm on to you. I know your game, lady. "Oh," he says. Like he's going to ask me where something is, and I'm not going to know. It's like I've got a schematic drawing in my head and each drawer is labeled. It's so simple. It's just like that. "Oh." So I turn to him. I'm going to say something. Something nice maybe. Maybe I won't say something nice, I don't know. So I turn to him with the knife still in my hand. But my back was to him before, you see. So I turn around with the knife. And maybe it has some blood on it. Maybe, I don't know. And he goes, "Aah!" Not "oh" this time, but "aah!" Not "aha!" like he just found the answer, like he remembered where the red handkerchief was, but "aah!" like he'd stubbed his toe, or caught a rose thorn in the thumb or something. Like he'd been stabbed. Maybe. How should I know? What does a man who has been stabbed sound like? That's not something you learn. So he makes this sound and then he goes running down the hall and locks himself in the bathroom.

Of course I follow him. With the knife. What kind of wife drops the knife when her husband makes a sound like that? So I follow him, and I'm outside the bathroom, and I'm listening. I hear calming sounds, the sound of running water. My mother used to do that when she was upset. She'd just sit in the bathroom and let the water run. Like a stream, she said. So he's running the water, I assume, because that's what I hear and some deep breathing, like you do at the doctor's office. And I'm knocking, and saying, "What's going on in there?" And I still have the knife in my right hand and I'm knocking with my left, asking what's going on. Because, what do I know? He could be dying in there for all I know, or he could be going to the bathroom. What else do you do in there? I guess he could be washing his face or something. But he's not that type. He's all business. If he's in there, there's a reason. I mean, he's breathing deeply, maybe he's having a heart attack. That's as good a place as any.

That explains the blood in the hallway. Blood from the lamb chops. I don't like to think about the little lambs, so I tell my kids they are just chops, you know, every animal has a chop. Personally I think of sheep, the smelly ones from the zoo. I mean, no one feels sad about them. They'd just as soon eat you as take grain from you hand. So you may as well eat them. Actually, maybe I'm thinking of the goats.

Then when he leaves the bathroom, he goes to lie on the couch in the living room. He doesn't feel well. It's probably something he ate. He was always skipping breakfast and drinking tons of coffee and then eating something stupid, like a hot dog, on the way home. And then he moans. So maybe he was in the bathroom because he had heartburn or something. I don't know when he leaves the bathroom, because I'm in the kitchen. I'm cutting the meat and then mixing things and putting things together for dinner. The house doesn't run itself, it doesn't just produce food, though the kids think that, of course. They think the food just appears on the table for them, like magic. Ask them to set the table and it's like you want them to perform some kind of mystical rite. Set the table? They think life just happens. But I know it doesn't. So I'm in the kitchen, doing this and that. I can hear him moaning on the couch, of course. He's moaning. Not the same sound, not the "aah!" like before but more like "ooh, ooh" over and over. He can really play up the suffering, really milk it. I'm sure he's uncomfortable, but he doesn't say so. And he hasn't even addressed my question about the red handkerchief. I think about it while I chop the meat. I have this big bowl of marinade and I'm chopping the meat and putting it in there. Then I cover it and put it back in the refrigerator for later. And then I have to do the vegetables and the potatoes, there's that to do, and unload the dishwasher. But I'm done with the laundry. So I listen to him moaning on the couch, and I still have the knife in my hand, so I go to the door of the kitchen and I say, "What is it?" Because I want to know. What is it that's making him moan that way? And he clutches his stomach and his face balls up, like agony. That's what I think. But still, there's this nagging question in the back of my mind, where's the handkerchief? Where did he put it? So I ask him again, but this time I go right up to him where he's lying on the couch. I put my face right up next to his and I whisper, "Where's the red handkerchief?" I say it real soft so as not to alarm him. He's bunched up, he seems to be in real pain. I still have the knife in the one hand. I'm not doing anything with it though, I'm just holding it, down. Maybe I had been holding it above him, maybe, before I bend down to whisper in his ear. That explains how the blood gets on his shirt. Maybe I flung some blood across the kitchen at him when I turned around before. Or maybe it got there by dripping.

And then he says, "What?" again. He's not a stupid man. What kind of man just keeps saying *what?* He knows what I'm talking about. The handkerchief. He hasn't forgotten. That picture that the kids took, he framed it and put it up on the mantle, like it was a real portrait, painted for the man of the house. So there it is, right there. Perhaps I get a bit upset. I don't mean to. I don't mean to drop it on the floor. But I do. Okay. Things fall all the time and break. It happens. You move on.

He just stays there on the couch, moaning. He won't stop. He just keeps making that same sound, over and over. I tell him to go into the bedroom. Then I tell him to go down to the basement and watch some TV. He won't go. I won't say I dragged him. How does a woman of my size drag a man of his size down the stairs? I mean, he's over six feet tall. He works out at the gym. And me? I carry laundry up and down those stairs, sure, three times a day. And I work the vacuum there. But a man? Can't be done. Besides, down there is his space. I don't go in there. I don't like the dark wood and how the leather couch smells like a dead animal. I prefer to stay upstairs, where a little sunlight shines in the window and I can look out at the yard and see the flowers blooming. That down there is his thing and he's welcome to it. Smells like sweat and death down there. I don't drag him, he just goes down there like I ask, so I don't have to hear him moaning, and he can watch some TV. And there's a bar down there, so he can fix himself a drink. Myself, I don't go much for that kind of thing, so I don't know what he keeps down there. Maybe some whiskey or scotch. He wants to smoke cigars, but I absolutely forbid it. No smoking in the house. My mother died of lung cancer, but she never smoked a day in her life. It was my dad who was the smoker, and he lived to be eighty-five. So that's how it is. He likes it down there, he said, away from the noise. He means the kids and their friends, always using the ice machine, which sounds like a jackhammer. So he goes down there and I can hear the TV up here, but I can't complain because it's better than listening to him moan.

I still have the knife. When I ask him, nicely, to please go downstairs if he's going to continue that moaning, I guess I still have the knife. But I don't jab with it, or gesture. I just have it, and I stand in the kitchen doorway and I say, please, won't you please go downstairs and then I won't have to hear your infernal moaning which sounds like a horse giving birth to an elephant. I mean, how much can one woman listen to? So I have the knife, and maybe I punctuate my sentence with it, making a kind of exclamation point in the air, but I'm a good distance away when I do it, and there is no way that my little line in the air could be seen as an attack. I mean, I just move it up and down, emphasizing my point, like, hey, listen here, I'm talking to you. And he does seem to listen, because that's when he goes downstairs. I don't know how he gets there, I assume he walks, because as soon as I'm done making my point, I turn around and go back to the kitchen.

The knife. I have the knife in my hand and I finish the meat. So I finish cutting the meat and I put it in the refrigerator, and then I wash the knife, I always do that, because if you don't, if you just leave it dirty in the sink, that dulls it, and then it's not sharp enough to cut anything. So you have to wash the knife right away, that's what I do. And I dry it and put it away. And that's where it is. The knife is right there, where I put it after I washed it.

When I'm done, I'm free to look for the red handkerchief. It's still bothering me, and I feel that if I just devote some time to it, I can find the red handkerchief. Things don't just disappear. They don't. Each thing is somewhere, even if the thing is concealed. Or if someone is concealing it from you. So I begin my search. I am very methodical. It has to be in the house, doesn't it? If it isn't in the house, then it's somewhere else, and I can't very well control that, can I? So I start with his dresser, and of course it isn't there. And then I go to his closet. Then the bathroom. He never keeps stuff in there, but if he wanted to hide it from me, isn't that where he would put it? Because I would never think to look there.

I don't know what he was doing. Watching TV I suppose. I can hear it drifting up from the basement. I can't hear any more moaning, but that's the point. For me not to hear the moaning.

I continue my search in the bathroom, and I look through every drawer. And it is disgusting. I mean, the things in here. There's old hair and dead skin and fingernail clippings and used cotton swabs. Who keeps such things? So I get out the bleach. To clean up. The bathroom is supposed to be the most hygienic room in the house. That room is all about cleanliness and order. I start with the top drawer and work my way down. It's simple enough. Just a bit of bleach and water, a clean rag, and you just wipe things up.

When I'm done with that, it's easy enough to do the kitchen. I already have the bleach out and the bucket. I get a new rag, of course. The bathroom is disgusting, but the kitchen is clean, I keep it clean. But if you have the bleach out and you've just been cutting meat, I mean, it makes perfect sense. I get the rag and I just do a quick swipe, just swish and it's done. It takes no time at all. There isn't a lot of mess. I just like to know that no one is going to get sick, from the meat on the counter, from the germs. So I clean the kitchen. Real fast. And an idea comes to me: the dirty rags. Because I have the dirty rags and I'm collecting them, from under the sink in the kitchen, and the ones

I had just used to clean. And I'm going to take them down to the laundry room, which is where you keep all the dirty stuff. That is, until it gets clean and then you bring it upstairs. But you can't keep the dirty stuff upstairs. That wouldn't be right.

I take the dirty rags and then I realize that if I wanted to hide something, something dirty, I would hide it with other dirty things. Like with like. And then, who knows, someone might wash it, without thinking maybe, maybe because they don't see the thing you had hidden, because you'd hidden it, and then maybe it gets washed and then it isn't dirty anymore. So maybe someone else washes away the evidence for you. That's when I go around the house and start collecting the dirty rags. I already have the ones from the bathroom, and then I get the ones from the kitchen. No surprises there. But then I go to get the ones from the garage. Sometimes he works in the garage, and I have a separate place for him to put those rags, because I don't want them mixing with the regular rags. In the garage, there's a little plastic pail for him to stash the rags. And wouldn't that be the perfect place? If you were trying to hide something from someone and that someone never went into the garage, that would be the perfect place, right?

I go in. I go right into the garage and dump the rags out. And guess what I find? With the old rags I'd made from his jeans and old t-shirts. Right in there. It has grease on it and something else. I can't say for sure if it's blood, but it could be. Who can say? So I take the rags and all the cloths soaked in bleach and I put them right into the washing machine. What's that saying, the men they work from sun to sun? Exactly. Just when I think I'm done with laundry for what, twenty-four hours, bam! More laundry. So I put everything in there, just cram it in, it's full and I run a load. But before I start it, before I can turn the water on, that's when I hear silence coming from the den. And that's what's so weird. It's never silent. First there's TV, there's always TV, and then when he's bored with that he's got that infernal music he likes to listen to. He says it takes him back. So it's the TV or the music. And sometimes that talk radio, with the yelling and the shouting. He loves that. He sits and laughs and laughs. At what, I have no idea. What's he laughing at? I don't know, honestly. But I don't hear a thing, nothing. Just silence. He's stopped moaning. So, finally, I think, he's stopped the moaning, he's feeling better.

And as I'm walking up the stairs, that's when I see the dirt on the carpet. That man always forgets to take his shoes off when he comes home. I tell him every time, leave them on the landing, but no, he won't have it. Either that or he's in such a hurry that he forgets. Maybe he had to hide it in the garage, so he was thinking about that and not about his shoes. But I just had the carpet cleaned. Not two weeks ago. So I get out the steam cleaner, this handy little thing I saw in a catalog once, I forget where, maybe on an airplane, you know, when you have nothing better to do than sit there and shop. I get that out and I clean the carpet on the stairs, and then I keep going, I do the landing downstairs and the landing up, why not? The carpet is a mess, full of germs and bacteria. I hate it. I mean, it came with the house, what are you going to do? But I hate it. It's a big sponge for filth. Honestly. I keep cleaning. I go down the hallway and into the bedroom. But then I stop. Because I see the clean clothes on the bed, and it reminds me of the load in the washing machine, which I put in the dryer.

And then I stop, and I call out to him in the den, "Honey?" Just like that. Not too loud, not too soft, just "honey?" And I think I hear a little warble from inside, a jumbled message, but it sounds like "well" or maybe "yelp" or something. But he sounds okay, so I leave him be. The kids aren't home yet, dinner is an hour off, at least, so I let him have his fun, whatever he's doing in there. Maybe he's reading. That wouldn't be usual, but maybe that's what he's doing. How would I know? He's in there, he's not moaning. Okay.

I remember dinner, and how the kids will be home in about an hour. From music classes and sports. And I like to have dinner ready, so we can eat and then they do their homework and then off to bed. Boom. No messing around. That's how it's done here. Because I need to have a little time at night. Some quiet where I can just do the crossword puzzle and have some tea, when I'm done working and the kids are in bed. The house gets quiet, like it's empty, but quieter. During the day when it is empty, the house hums, as if the space needs something to fill it. But when it's full, the house is happy, content. So then the house settles down. And then I can just sit for a minute and not think about anything, just have some tea and like that.

I start fixing dinner, then, taking the meat out, letting it sit, making a salad, putting on the potatoes. Getting everything ready. When the kids get home, then I'll put the meat on, it only takes a few minutes. While they're telling me about their days. I always expect a complete report, who they talked to, what they did, what their teachers said, information such as that, while they were telling me about that stuff, then I could cook the meat and then dinner would be ready and then he would come up from the den. He always hears when the kids come home, and then he comes up about fifteen minutes later and that's when we eat. He always knows.

But when the kids come home, they're somber. Bad days all around. No goals in soccer, mistakes in violin lessons. Sourpuss. That's what I call them when they scowl. Sourpuss. So I set out the salad and put the meat on. And I'm waiting. I'm listening to their stories, their tales of woe, but honestly, aren't they always the same? The stories? I did this, then I did that. And it's all how you react. I tell them, but kids don't listen. They treat me like the hired help. Sure they want the hugs and the allowance. But they don't listen to the wisdom I have. I've earned this wisdom, through these years that I've cleaned up after them and washed their clothes. I pay attention, even when they're not paying attention to me. I listen. So I know what I'm talking about. They're telling me about their days, and we wait. They sit at the kitchen bar and drink their chocolate milk and we wait. Fifteen minutes, he's still not up. In my head, I swear, but I don't say anything aloud. I would never say those words in front of the children. They don't need to hear that.

So I ask them to go downstairs and get him. "Tell him to get up here for dinner," I say. "Tell him now."

They go downstairs, and I check the meat. It's leaking red juice and getting brown. Almost done. And I'm waiting. I'm always waiting. Nothing ever happens when it should. I have to wait and wait.

That's when I hear them call from downstairs. They say he's lying on the couch.

"Wake him up," I yell. "Tell him to get up here!" I'm mad now, of course, because he's sleeping and it's dinner time. I mean honestly. If he didn't stay up all night doing god knows what, then he wouldn't be so tired. So I tell them to get him up here.

Now the meat is burning and I have to take it off, and I almost burn my hand. And the kids are yelling now, yelling for me to come down. Well, I don't go down there. Finally they come up and say he's not sleeping. Maybe he's not breathing.

Well, either he's breathing or he's not. So we discuss this. Is he breathing or not? Is he not breathing?

They plead with me, tell me to go get him. He needs help. What am I going to do? I'm just a woman who debones lamb chops and broils them. Who makes dinner and gets it on the table, no fooling around. That's my job.

"I can't help him," I say. "How can I help him?" For a minute, I picture the red handkerchief, spinning and turning in the dryer, hot, too hot to touch, just spinning there, weightless almost. It's perfectly clean, without a trace of what happened. The handkerchief doesn't remember. It's perfectly blank.